TEARS OF THE DRAGON

Angelique Anjou

Fantasy Romance

New Concepts   Georgia

Be sure to check out our website for the very best in fiction at fantastic prices!

When you visit our webpage, you can:

* Read excerpts of currently available books
* View cover art of upcoming books and current releases
* Find out more about the talented artists who capture the magic of the writer's imagination on the covers
* Order books from our backlist
* Find out the latest NCP and author news--including any upcoming book signings by your favorite NCP author
* Read author bios and reviews of our books
* Get NCP submission guidelines
* And so much more!

We offer a 20% discount on all new ebook releases!
(Sorry, but short stories are not included in this offer.)

We also have contests and sales regularly, so be sure to visit our webpage to find the best deals in ebooks and paperbacks! To find out about our new releases as soon as they are available, please be sure to sign up for our newsletter (http://www.newconceptspublishing.com/newsletter.htm) or join our reader group (http://groups.yahoo.com/group/new_concepts_pub/join) !

The newsletter is available by double opt in only and our customer information is *never* shared!

Visit our webpage at:
www.newconceptspublishing.com

Tears of the Dragon is an original publication of NCP. This work has never before appeared in book form. This work is a novel. Any similarity to actual persons or events is purely coincidental.

New Concepts Publishing
5202 Humphreys Rd.
Lake Park, GA 31636

ISBN 1-58608-705-3
© copyright 2004 Angelique Anjou
Cover art by Jenny Dixon, © copyright 2004

NCP books are available at special quantity discounts for bulk purchases for sales promotions, premiums, fund raising, or educational use. For details, write, email, or phone New Concepts Publishing, 5202Humphreys Rd., Lake Park, GA 31636, ncp@newconceptspublishing.com, Ph. 229-257-0367, Fax 229-219-1097.

First NCP Paperback Printing: 2005

Printed in the United States of America

Other Titles from NCP by Angelique Anjou:

Dream Warriors
Ja-Rael's Lioness

Chapter One

Lennie nudged his partner. "That's her, comin' down the steps."

"Which one?" Tony peered through the gathering gloom.

Lennie glared at him. "The dame, ya moron."

"My eyes ain't so good after dark," Tony said sulkily. "An' anyway, she was behind the hulking giant there. I thought you was talkin' 'bout one of them dames over there by the sidewalk."

"Them's workin' girls, numb nuts. Just get the damned trunk open," Lennie growled, crawling out of the car as the petite redhead reached the sidewalk, bid the man who was with her good evening and turned in their direction.

She was a pretty little thing, Lennie thought as she came closer and he was able to make out her features … delicate … like one of them china dolls, but with curves in all the right places. It was a pure waste to whack a dame that looked that good. He didn't like doing dames anyway. It offended him, almost as bad as having to whack a kid. He wondered what she'd done to tick his boss off.

Shrugging it off, he stepped away from the car when she came abreast of him. "S'cuse me, ma'am? I wonder if you could point me in the direction of 110th street?"

The woman paused, looked him over curiously. "This is 110th," she said in surprise.

He looked around, saw no one was looking in their direction and grabbed her, covering her mouth with his hand as he hauled her off her feet and moved to the trunk of the car, which was open and waiting, Tony nervously fingering the lid.

The woman, Lennie noticed, had gone limp in his arms the moment he'd grabbed her. He wasn't falling for that one though. Dropping her into the trunk, he stuffed a gag in her mouth, tied it with quick efficiency, and trussed her like a Thanksgiving turkey. The whole job took less than five minutes, but Tony looked like he was going to pee on himself as he danced around the rear of the car.

"You need to take a leak, or what?" Lennie snarled as he slammed the trunk lid.

"I don't like grabbin' her right here in the street. No tellin' who might've seen it. We shoulda waited, like I said, till she was close to an alley."

Lennie gave him a look. "Get in the car, moron. She don't walk by no alley. She catches a cab at the corner and hits for home. I been watchin' her for a week."

"What'er we gonna do now?" Tony asked nervously, once they were settled in the car again.

"We go to the docks. Where else?"

"What ya got in mind?"

"Somethin' quiet. I figured we could tie a brick to her or somethin' and pitch her over the side. Boss didn't say to get rid of the body, but he likes things tidy, so I figure he'll be happier if we don't leave it layin' around."

"She sure is pretty," Tony said wistfully.

"Yeah? And how would you know? You didn't even know which dame I was talkin' about."

"Think we got time to get a little honey before we snuff her?"

Lennie gave him a look. "Hey! She's a lady. Didn't your mudder teach you no manners? You don't get fresh with ladies."

Tony gaped at him. "But … but … we're gonna snuff the dame!"

"That's different. It ain't personal. We're just doin' our job here. An' our job ain't about rapin' and pilagin'. It's about makin' the boss's problems disappear. Besides, foolin' around is dangerous." He shook his head. "We off her. We tie an anchor to her and we ditch her."

* * * *

Khalia Peterson couldn't decide whether the discussion, which was perfectly audible to her in the trunk, was intended to scare her or if they didn't realize, or didn't care, that she could hear them.

She was irritated, regardless. She *was* a lady. They had no business manhandling her in such a way. They'd ruined her coiffure! Her suit was probably ruined, as well, and she'd just bought it the week before. The trunk stank of chemicals and the lord only knew what else.

What really ticked her off, though, was that they'd put her in the position of having to complete the destruction of her lovely suit. She'd been thinking it over ever since they'd tossed her into the trunk. The big ox that had grabbed her had said they were headed for the docks, which meant she might have twenty minutes to come up with an alternative.

Unfortunately, she couldn't think of one.

Sighing, trying to tamp her justifiable anger, she concentrated on shifting.

She must have concentrated for a full ten minutes. All the while, she was jounced unmercifully in the trunk as her kidnappers seemed to go out of their way to find every stinking pothole between 110th and the docks, until she began to think she must know what it felt like to be a basketball.

Nothing happened and her confidence began to seep insidiously away as the sound of heavy traffic faded and they drew nearer their destination. Resolutely, she ignored the gradual siphoning of her assurance. She'd always prided herself on her clear-head in the face of disaster, her ability to calmly assess any situation and pursue the most logical course.

She had first learned that she could shift when she'd reached puberty. It wasn't a 'gift' that she'd found a great deal of use for, however, and, if she were honest with herself, she wasn't particularly thrilled at the ability to become a female of Amazonian proportions merely by willing it. There were certainly drawbacks to being a small person, but weren't there always drawbacks with everything? And she rather liked being referred to as petite. In her mind, it made up for some of her other shortcomings--her garish, blindingly red hair, for instance.

She supposed now, though, that she might ought to have practiced her gift in case of need. She needed it now, if she ever had, and she couldn't seem to recall how she'd summoned it before.

Taking a deep breath, she closed her mind to the tell tale thump of the tires over wooden planks that told her they'd reached the docks and concentrated once more, her mind focused on the discomfort of having her hands tied behind her back.

Even as the car slowed and abruptly rocked to a halt, she felt a tingle in her hands and arms, then the burning sensation as bones and muscle lengthened and stretched, bursting the sleeves of her jacket and then the rope around her wrists.

It was heartening, but hardly enough. Two huge arms weren't going to be enough to fight off two men with guns.

As she heard the doors slam and the footfalls of the men coming around to the back of the car, she thought of the amulet she always wore next to her heart, the dragon's tear.

They were after it. That had to be the reason behind this and 'the boss' they'd referred to none other than Clyde Hawkins. He'd approached her only the week before regarding the legend of the tear, hinting that he suspected she had it in her possession.

Digging it from her bodice, she clutched the tear possessively. It was all that she had from the mother she'd never known. She wouldn't part from it for any price. She wasn't about to allow these hooligans to steal it from her.

To her relief, as if merely holding the amulet tightly in her fist were enough to focus her gift, she felt her body growing, transforming, heard the tear of fabric and bursting seams. The moment the catch of the trunk clicked, she rolled onto her knees and thrust upward, exploding out of the trunk and bowling both men over.

She checked, tempted to make use of her size and strength to teach the men the error of their ways, but her size did not make her proof against bullet holes and the surprise hadn't lasted long. She'd barely cleared them when the two men began scrambling for their guns. Whirling, she fled toward the edge of the dock, launching herself toward the water even as she felt the first barrage of bullets whiz past her.

She hit--something--even as she launched herself off the pier. Her mind, grasping to assimilate the unknown, produced the sensation of swimming through a chilled, clinging jell. Briefly, the air seemed to be sucked from her lungs. Sound ceased. Even as an unfamiliar sense of panic touched her mind, however, her struggle to gasp was suddenly rewarded by a sharp intake of breath. The sensation of traveling at high velocity was as instantaneous as the breath of air.

Expecting to feel the chill wetness of water, Khalia was so stunned when her fingers plowed the warm graininess of sand that that stunned her almost as much as the impact of her body against solid earth. Fortunately, she regained the ability to move at about the same instant that she was finally able to draw breath into her lungs again. Sneezing and coughing, she turned her head to try to drag in a breath free of airborne debris and finally managed to climb to her knees.

The belly flop in the sand dune had knocked her 'shift' out of her as well as the air from her lungs. The tattered remains of her clothing fluttered in the sharp breeze blowing over her, pieces drifting downward and settling to the ground around her along with the debris she'd plowed up from the desert floor.

It was a desert, she realized the moment she managed to wipe enough sand from her eyes to peer around her. She hadn't imagined the sand, or the friction burns on her palms, her knees, and, in fact, pretty much everything in between. Her clothing had protected her somewhat in more tender areas, but, as she'd known would happen, shifting had pretty well shredded her clothing, leaving a lot more exposed skin than might have been vulnerable otherwise.

When she'd assured herself she was alone, she spat the grit from her mouth. Spitting in public was incredibly unladylike and ill-mannered, and she was embarrassed to *think* about doing it, let alone *do* it. On the other hand, she couldn't believe it would be very healthful to swallow dirt and, since no one seemed to be about to witness the lapse, she was more interested in her health and comfort at the moment than a lapse in manners. When she'd expelled as much of the grit as she possibly could, she sat back and looked around a little dazedly, absently shaking the sand from a tattered bit of clothing and using it to blot her lips.

The glow of a full moon lit her surroundings. As far as she could see in every direction, there was nothing but rolling dunes. In the moonlight, the sand looked as if it had the color and consistency of brick dust.

Where was the city? And how had she come to find herself in a desert of all places? The city was surrounded by marsh and water, not desert.

Khalia was still trying to assimilate the indigestible when a dark shadow swooped above her head. Ducking instinctively, Khalia's head whipped toward the perceived threat. She was arrested, however, by a sight that so took her by surprise that she could only blink at it, stunned, unable to think at all.

A pair of moons had just crested the horizon. Even as she glanced up to see what had produced the light overhead that she'd assumed was a full moon, a man landed in the sand barely two yards away from her.

He was the next thing to naked. For several horrifying moments, she thought he was completely naked, but even as her eyes dropped with a will of their own toward his genitals, a tiny bit of relief trickled through her. *That*, at least, was covered, not decently, for she could not consider that pouch that so obviously was only sufficient to hold his genitalia as decent, but covered in a way that prevented yet another jolt to her already overloaded sensibilities. Nevertheless, all that bare flesh was so shocking that her mind simply ceased to function for several moments.

Dropping to one knee, he struck his left breast with his right fist, bowing his head. "Your highness! We rejoice that you have at last returned to us. I am Damien Bloodragon, King Caracus' champion, sent to protect you."

Chapter Two

Khalia found herself repeating the words over and over, trying to make sense of what he'd said. By the fourth repetition, it occurred to her that he'd mistaken her for someone else. The question was, would it be safer to lie and pretend she was that person? Or to admit she wasn't whomever he'd mistaken her for?

With an effort, she gathered enough moisture into her mouth to speak. Honesty, she'd found, was always the best policy. "I've never been here before in my life--where ever here is."

He lifted his head, studied her a long moment and finally saluted again. "I beg pardon for my clumsiness, Princess. I should have said, we rejoice that you have come home at last."

Her lips tightened. With an effort, she got to her feet, trying to cover her own nakedness with the tattered remains of her clothing. "This can't be home. I've never been here before in my life!"

There was desperation, and perhaps even just a tiny hint of hysteria in her voice. It embarrassed her, but, really, she thought she might be forgiven for a little slip considering all that she'd experienced since she'd left the museum.

He stood as she did, revealing something she'd failed to notice before. He towered over her alarmingly. Shadows cloaked him like a thin veil, despite the moons' illumination, but not enough for her peace of mind. The light glinted off of bulging muscles on his arms, his chest and torso, and even his legs. It also gleamed off of spiked metal epaulets on his shoulders, and the pierced metal bands that protected his ribs. A dark cloak fluttered in the wind behind him, but otherwise he wore nothing but gauntlets, leggings, the obscene cod piece, and a head dress that looked like the skull of a dragon, complete with lethal looking teeth.

Overall, he made her insides shimmy like the jell-like substance she vaguely recalled falling through when she'd tried to dive from the pier.

Seemingly of their own accord, her eyes flicked over the cod piece once more, drawn, perhaps, by movement there? She wasn't certain, but the moment her gaze slid over the cod piece, it grew significantly, alarmingly, larger.

"It is the home of your ancestors, Princess. The home world of your mother, her royal highness, Princess Rheaia."

She might have been able to compose herself somewhat if he hadn't mentioned the mother she'd never known, but whom she knew most definitely was not a princess. The fact that he mentioned 'home world' … as if she had found herself on a world other than her own brought entirely different emotions into play, however.

All things considered, she decided the man must be dangerously deranged. The thought had no more than registered in her mind than, without any effort whatsoever, she shifted, towering over him.

She was pleased with herself for all of two seconds. He completely stunned her when he shifted as well, once more towering over her as he had before.

She gaped at the grim smile that curled his lips.

"And thus, all doubt is removed. You can not be other than the princess, or you would not have the ability to shift … come. We dare not linger here, in the land of your enemies. I must take you to Caracaren."

Retreat suddenly seemed the better part of valor. Khalia took a step back. "Sir! You are mistaken! My name is Khalia--Khalia Peterson and I don't know any Princess Rheaia and I'm not about to go anywhere with you!" Whirling, she fled. She hadn't managed to make much headway up the nearest dune, however, when he flattened her.

The impact of having him land on top of her resulted in much the same shock as she'd experienced when she had executed the grand belly flop on the sand in her first dive. His body crushed the air from her lungs.

"Your pardon, princess. But I must insist!" he growled as he rolled off of her and grasped her around the waist, lifting her from the ground.

When Khalia finally managed to clear her vision enough to look up at him, it was immediately apparent that she hadn't merely imagined the growth of his male member. The pupils of his eyes as he gazed down at her were dilated until only a thin, almost purple halo separated the iris from the white of his eyes. His skin was flushed, his nostrils flared and quivering with each ragged breath.

She hardly thought capturing her had required enough expenditure of energy to account for his physical distress. She didn't flatter herself that she was either so beautiful or alluring that it was merely her wonderful self that had evoked such a reaction. On the other hand, he was a man-- she supposed--certainly a male anyway, and she was the next thing to indecent in her tattered clothing. Perhaps her near nakedness and her attempt to flee had been sufficient in itself to arouse the hunter in him?

It had been poor judgment on her part to attempt flight when she had no safe haven to flee to, the sort of silly, useless effort a brainless female might try, not one like herself who prided herself on her intelligence and cool head.

Unfortunately, despite her certainty that she possessed both, she was still a female, and her own body responded to the desire she sensed in him more swiftly even than her mind could assess it.

"You are in season," he growled through gritted teeth, his tone almost accusing.

Khalia gaped at him, feeling her cheeks turn scarlet. "I beg your pardon!" she gasped indignantly when she finally found her voice. "I'm a woman. Not a … a mare!"

He had lifted his head, however, and she had the distinct feeling he scarcely registered either her remarks or her outrage. "If there is another male within miles. … Hell and damnation!"

As abruptly as he'd grabbed her, he thrust her behind him. Khalia was so stunned that it wasn't until she'd peered around him that she saw the man drop to the sand a few yards away. She stared at the newest arrival blankly. What sort of insane place was this anyway that men dropped from the sky like hail?

Glancing up, she saw two dark shapes rapidly moving in their direction. At first, she thought it was huge birds. As they drew nearer, however, she saw that it was winged men--winged male creatures she amended as they hovered briefly just above. Abruptly, the wings vanished and they, too, dropped to the sand. "Mercy!"

"Stay close behind me--but not too close," Damien growled.

Before she could demand to know how she was supposed to follow such a command, assuming she wanted to, a patch of red, scaly hide popped through the smooth flesh that covered his back. Rippling and moving like a live thing, it consumed him, replacing the flesh of his entire body--all that she could see of it--within moments. Along his spine, sharp, pointed ridges of bone protruded almost like jagged teeth. From his shoulder blades emerged dark, leathery extrusions which expanded and lengthened before they unfurled, looking like nothing so much as the wings of a giant bat.

She came as close to fainting as she ever had in her life when he turned his head to give her a warning glance. The face of manly beauty that had captivated her attention had vanished. In its place was the head of a demon creature.

She was still rooted to the ground in horror when he arched his neck and spit a wall of flame at the three 'challengers' who faced him. Gripped in the trance-like state of shock, her gaze followed the leaping, curling wall of flame even while her brain screamed at her not to look, envisioning scorched flesh melting from bones as the flames licked it. A jolt went through her as she saw the other 'men.'

They weren't men at all, but rather half man half beast-- much like the man who called himself Damien Bloodragon, except that Damien was no longer a man at all. All vestiges of man had vanished from him she realized when he charged forward to attack the man-beasts.

She wasn't certain how long she remained rooted to the same spot, watching the deadly dance of the four men in horror as they slashed and bit at each other with razor sharp claws and teeth, belching fire and smoke, but it could not be said that her brain finally kicked in and began to work once more. Like a scratched phonograph record, a few words filtered through her mind and, sluggishly, her mind began to decipher the meanings. In the end, however, it was more the primal urge of survival that moved her almost mechanically across the dunes. 'Tunnel--home' kept repeating through her mind over and over, as if the phonograph needle had stuck in one spot.

It was a desert landscape. There was little enough to serve as landmarks and the men-beasts had torn up the sand in their deadly battle--she refused to think of the implications of Damien Bloodragon's remark about her being 'in season' only moments before the others had appeared, but escape was uppermost in her mind as she began to make her way slowly around the battle in search of the spot where she'd landed when she'd emerged from the strange tunnel.

She had not traversed half the distance between the spot where Damien had left her and the spot she decided must have been her entrance into this bizarre world, when one of the creatures landed solidly in front of her. The stench of scorched flesh hit her like a slap in the face, effectively lifting her from much of the shock that had numbed her. Almost like a sleepwalker awakening in a place far removed from where they had laid their head to sleep, she blinked, her mind opening to a blast of perceptions at once.

Blood seeped from dozens of wounds on his body--the body of some creature not humanoid, but rather reptilian. Scales covered parts of his body, like armor, but so too, did more human-like flesh, though much of that was burned. His head was grotesquely deformed, not quite human, and not quite reptilian, but somewhere between the two.

As he took a step toward her and Khalia's whole body tensed for flight, she was gripped suddenly by a clawed hand that encircled her entire waist. Her head whipped instinctively toward the newest threat.

The dragon who held her leaned toward her until they were almost nose to nose. "I told you to stay back," he muttered in a rumbling, growling hiss.

Before Khalia could do more than gape at him, he set her behind him and gave her a push to urge her out of the way as he met the beast that had threatened her. In all fairness, she supposed he believed it a 'gentle' push. The fact of the matter was, however, that he was far stronger than a human. She flew backward several feet before she hit the ground and rolled down a dune. Still stunned, she rolled to her knees within moments of coming to a halt and began scrambling toward her goal once more, more desperately than before.

As mind boggling as the entire incident was, as difficult as it was to register all that had been happening, she'd still noted the two bodies lying in the sand, dying or dead already. Damien and the remaining man beast were locked in battle now. One would win. She was fairly certain she wanted nothing to do with whoever won and she was running out of time and options.

Closing her mind to the growls, roars and meaty thuds as they pounded at each other, she searched frantically along the dune for the tunnel she had never actually seen. She had felt it though and she reasoned that she should be able to feel it again if she found it.

She came up empty. Glancing around a little desperately to get her bearings, she noticed two things almost simultaneously. The creature that Damien had become had vanquished his foe … and she was standing, as nearly as she could tell, where she'd landed when she'd found herself in the desert. As the great beast rose and looked around for her, she stumbled to her feet, gathered herself and, clutching the amulet as she had before, she dove.

She felt certain she plowed up three feet of sand when she touched down like an airplane coming in for a landing-- minus landing gear. The air being pounded from her lungs on impact was all that kept the cloud of dust she dug up from saturating her throat and lungs. Even so, she was coughing when an arm snaked around her waist and jerked her to her feet.

"You can not return to the other world."

"I wasn't trying to," Khalia lied when she managed to catch her breath, batting the sand from her eyes with her lashes and finally peering up at him.

He was--he looked--human once more, but she knew better now and she didn't feel any less threatened.

One dark brow arched skeptically, but he said nothing for several moments, lifting his head to scan the skies above them. "I should have realized at once that you were in season and the danger far worse than I'd anticipated."

Despite her fear of the creature, Khalia felt indignation rise once more. "That is a vile, disgusting thing to say! If I wasn't a lady, I'd slap your face!"

He looked at her, his eyes narrowing, but in a moment the corners of his mouth twitched, a smile threatening. He curbed the urge when she glared at him, though his eyes still gleamed with amusement and something else she rather preferred not to interpret. "Your pardon, princess. It was merely a statement of fact and not intended to insult you."

His audacity bereft her of speech for perhaps two heartbeats. "It is NOT a fact," she snapped. "I am a woman … human. We do not go into he-- We do not come in sea--"

Both dark brows lifted that time. Instead of releasing her, however, he moved his hands to her upper arms. Grasping them firmly, he hauled her closer, dipping his head until they were almost nose to nose. It wasn't until that moment that Khalia realized that he wasn't gasping from exertion so much as the effort to control his urges. His eyes were dark with hunger and as he dragged in a deep breath, his features hardened. A tremor traveled through the hands that gripped her.

As before, and despite all logic to the contrary, her body instantly responded to the desire she sensed in him. It moved over and through her like a wave of electricity, making her skin prickle with hypersensitivity. Abruptly, she was aware of her own body in a way she never had been before and him as she had never been aware of another man. The heat of his body, his scent, his sheer male magnificence rolled over her, annihilating the last shreds of her common sense.

"Your scent is as delicate as a lotan blossom and as fiery as acid in my blood. If I were not disciplined to ignore my primal urges because of my position in caring for the royal family, I would have taken you myself. Not one male within a twenty mile radius can resist your allure at this moment. I must take you some place safe until your time has passed ... or you will have no choice in your mate, for the strongest will take you."

He might have been speaking gibberish for all Khalia understood. His husky voice slid along her nerve endings like the caress of a hand, sending warming, pleasurable, knee weakening vibrations throughout her body. She sighed, unconsciously lifting her lips a little closer in silent supplication.

She wasn't certain when he ceased speaking and his gaze focused on her mouth, but the rush of his breath, as if a giant hand had suddenly squeezed the air from his lungs, escalated want to need and she leaned infinitesimally closer.

"Olgin's balls!" he growled, setting her away from him abruptly. "You tempt me to your peril, princess. I am a soldier first. But I am still a man."

Khalia blinked in surprise, but it was several moments before the obvious crudity/curse filtered through her heated brain and several more before the implications of his last comment made a connection. She gaped at him in outrage then, revolted by the very notion that she was so lost to all sense of propriety as to encourage any man, let alone a ... savage to think that she was eager for his lovemaking, making no attempt to hide either her outrage or her revulsion. "I tempt ... *I*!" she stammered. "Your ... primal urges have fried your brain, you ... you ... whatever sort of creature you are!"

His features hardened with anger. He caught her wrists this time, slowly and deliberately forcing them behind her back until she was forced to arch her back to relieve the pressure. Manacling both her wrists with one hand, he just as deliberately flicked the tatters of her jacket aside and cupped one of her breasts, pinching the erect bud at the end. Something very like a jolt of electricity went through her, but she wasn't certain, at first, if it was purely from shock at his familiarity or something else entirely. When he lowered his head and replaced his fingers with his mouth, lathing the sensitive tip with his tongue and then covering it with his mouth and suckling, she lost all awareness of anything beyond the mindless pleasure that enveloped her, weakening her knees, constricting the air in her lungs until she found herself struggling to breathe.

"I am dragon … just as you are, princess," he growled when he lifted his head at last.

Khalia struggled to lift her eyelids and focus on what he was saying. "I am no such thing. My parents were human beings … not … not."

"Dragons?" he supplied, his eyes narrowed now, his breath as ragged as her own. "Your sire was human. Your mother, Princess Rheaia, was as I am--Dragon. But do not despair, sheashona. I will not hold it against you that you are only a half breed."

Chapter Three

Khalia strongly suspected that Damien had transformed himself into a dragon merely for the purpose of intimidating her. If he had needed only the ability of flight, she had seen that he could achieve that merely by producing wings at will, so she could only consider his shift from man to fearsome beast as premeditated and for that purpose alone.

It had worked, but she was not so spineless as to allow him to know. In any case, he had grabbed her up and taken flight without so much as a 'by your leave' and it had taken her quite some time to adapt to the sensation.

She had witnessed the acrobatics of a biplane on several occasions--it was 1920 after all and everyone seemed convinced by now that airplanes were the future of transport--but she had certainly not been foolhardy enough to climb into one--if man had been intended to fly, he would have been born with wings--and had never anticipated the possibility, or desire, of doing so. To find herself suddenly whisked into the sky had been a traumatizing experience, and she wasn't altogether certain but what the long term effects upon a person's health would prove to be detrimental. She was convinced that the heart palpitations it had caused her already could not be considered a good thing.

Fortunately, they had not been airborne long before, in the distance, she noticed what at first appeared to be a jutting of rock on the very edge of the desert. Damien, she realized was flying directly toward it, for within moments they drew close enough that she could make out the regular angles and twisted spires that denoted a manmade--dragonmade? --non-naturally occurring formation. Before they had gotten close enough for Khalia to make out much in the way of details, however, a dozen or so 'dots' rose from it, like a swarm of angry bees, and headed directly toward them.

Remembering the dragon men Damien had had to fight off of her, Khalia was instantly terrorized and it was only by sheer willpower that she managed to keep a stiff upper lip in the face of what appeared to be almost certain death. Not for a moment did she believe these beasts could sense anything except, possibly, that she was a female, but it seemed a moot point when *they* were convinced that she was ripe for mating.

She had always prided herself on her imagination. Next to her intelligence, she had thought it a most profound gift, for it allowed her to view the bits and pieces of ancient civilizations that arrived at the museum and visualize the civilization that had created them.

Unfortunately, at the moment, it also allowed her to visualize an aerial battle between a dozen and one primal creatures bent on being first to mate with the female Damien had discovered…. And her lifeless body splattered on the ground below while they continued to slug it out, unaware that they'd 'broken' the prize they were all fighting over.

For the first time in her life she perfectly understood the look of abject terror on the face of female dogs she'd seen racing before a pact of determined males.

"Mercy!" she exclaimed when she managed to collect enough spit in her mouth to unglue her tongue from the roof.

She was glad she had refrained from screaming in horror. She'd no sooner uttered the single word when an insect struck the corner of her mouth with the velocity of a shotgun pellet, proof positive that self-restraint was its own reward.

"It is the royal guard," Damien growled at her in that deep, gravelly voice that emerged from his dragon's chest.

"Oh?" she managed, pardonably pleased with herself that the single word seemed almost regally aloof, rather than doubtful, or even relieved.

"Let us hope that they are as disciplined as I had thought."

"No! Don't spare me the bad news. I can take it," Khalia said dryly.

He made a sound that might have been a chuckle, or a snort, she wasn't certain which, but the attempt at humor didn't particularly lighten her own mood.

The group of dragon men stopped well before they reached Damien and Khalia, hovering, it seemed to Khalia, indecisively, their great wings stirring the hot air from the desert below. Not so much as a single word passed between them and Khalia was surprised when the soldiers abruptly saluted in the same manner that Damien had saluted her and then fell in around and behind them. She glanced at Damien curiously. As if he sensed her gaze, he tilted his head.

It was uncanny, really, that the eyes watching her from that massive dragon head were so exactly the same as Damien's eyes. They were even the strange, almost purple color of Damien's eyes. One would have thought the man would disappear completely once the beast had taken over.

"You have no understanding of dragon folk."

It was not a question, rhetorical or otherwise, but there was censure in the comment, Khalia felt certain. She might have ignored the remark except that he'd already spoken insultingly of her being a half breed. She responded to the disapproval therefore even though it irritated her that she felt provoked. Why should she care what his opinion of her was anyway? She was an exceptionally well educated woman. She'd not only graduated from high school, she'd graduated from a women's college, as well. "You'll have to forgive my ignorance. They didn't teach it in my school."

He merely grunted, which was almost as annoying as the remark had been to begin with. She would've felt better if she'd seen some sign that her sarcasm was at least as irritating to him as his bigotry was to her.

"Princess Rheaia should have seen to it that you were better prepared."

Khalia sent him a cold look. "If my mother was Princess Rheaia, as you seem to believe, then she could hardly be faulted for not preparing me since she died at my birth," Khalia lied without remorse. She didn't for a moment believe her mother had been this Princess Rheaia that he kept referring to, and she knew very well that her mother had not died in child bed--she had, for reasons Khalia had never been privy to, given Khalia up for adoption--but she wasn't about to let some complete stranger insult her mother!

The dragon Damien frowned, but it was far more thoughtful than annoyed. "Your pardon. You may rest assured, however, that she would never have given you up unless she feared for your safety, sheashona."

Khalia sent him a startled glance and then frowned, wondering if she'd mentioned that she'd grown up in an orphanage, but she could not believe that she had. She'd never told anyone. Had she, somehow, given herself away?

Before she could decide how to respond to the remark, Damien settled on the ramparts of the castle and released her. Around them, the other man-beasts landed, shifting into perfectly ordinary looking men.

Upon consideration, Khalia mentally revived the assessment. They looked like perfectly extraordinary men, well built, handsome--and as bizarrely garbed as her captor, Damien. Nevertheless, she would never have believed that they were other than men if she had not seen them shift from beast to man.

To her discomfort, they knelt and saluted as Damien had. She was still wondering what to say, or if there was something she should say, when Damien grasped her arm and led her from the ramparts and into the fortress.

Although more ancient civilizations were her forte`, her position in the museum, if not her extensive education, had made her somewhat familiar with the medieval period of Europe. She was conversant enough in any case that she immediately noticed that the fortress bore little resemblance to any castle she'd ever studied. It was definitely not new, but neither ancient, nor primitive. The exterior appeared to be constructed entirely of some sort of stone that bore a strong resemblance to slate. She had no idea what the probability might be of stone from her own world occurring naturally on another, but the properties of slate, which was that it was highly resistant to fire, seemed to indicate a strong probability that it had at least that much in common with slate. As they approached the massive door that opened off of the ramparts, it swung open without a sound, belching a gust of chilled air.

Khalia checked when she saw no one stood in the portal, but Damien urged her on without even glancing at the door. Glancing back, she saw it swing closed behind them just as quickly and quietly. Frowning, she looked around the corridor they found themselves in. The walls were made of the same material as the exterior. The ceiling was one continuous arch from end to end. She saw neither gaslights nor electric bulbs, no candles, no torches in wall sconces, and yet a soft light enveloped them as they traversed the long corridor, appearing before them, disappearing behind them.

They had walked for some time when Damien stopped before a set of arched double doors. Unlike the previous door, this one remained closed. Khalia looked at Damien questioningly.

"General Damien Bloodragon and Princess Khalia, daughter of Princess Rheaia."

Khalia looked around to see whom he might be speaking to, but saw no one, nor even any sort of mechanical marvel such as those Edison had devised. Instead, a strange blue band of light appeared, traveled their length and up again.

The doors swung inward silently. With little more than a faint flicker, the room illuminated. Releasing his hold on her arm at last, Damien strode inside. "These are the royal apartments. They have not been occupied since your grandfather's time. The usurper was not inclined to visit the outlying provinces himself." He looked around the room and frowned. "It is antiquated and cramped, but you should be comfortable enough here until … it is safe to travel."

Khalia realized as he turned to her that she was staring in awestruck wonder. Embarrassed at the thought of being caught gaping like a hayseed, she quickly assumed a look of polite interest. She'd heard very little of what he'd said, however, too stunned by the magnificence of the room to do anything but gawk at the rich tapestries, gilded furniture, jewel encrusted vases. Even the floor was covered with thick, beautiful carpets.

Acutely aware of her state, she remained on the threshold, certain she could feel sand dropping from her with each breath she took.

"You will want to freshen up." He held out his hand. "If you will come this way, I will show you the facilities. Your pardon, princess. There are no servants to attend you, but I gladly offer my services … if you will allow."

Khalia merely stared at him, not entirely certain whether that was a question or not, or precisely what it was that he was offering. She'd been on the point of asking for water to bathe, but when he mentioned facilities it occurred to her that, in all probability, the fortress boasted indoor plumbing. That thought propelled her forward at last and she followed him to a smaller set of double doors. These swung open at their approach as the first door had, illuminating to reveal a bedchamber that rivaled the previous room in opulence. The bed alone was approximately the size of the bedroom in her tiny apartment in the city. Elevated on a platform, two tiered steps approached it. Sheer draperies were attached to a circular canopy above the center of the bed and fell in swags which were tied to each of the four corner posts.

Beyond the bed, the room was surprisingly sparsely furnished. A long vanity with a mirror above it and a padded stool before it sat along one wall on one side and a pair of comfortable looking, overstuffed chairs faced a small, low table on the other side of the bed.

Several moments passed before Khalia realized that Damien was standing patiently beside another pair of arched double doors, these only slightly wider than a single, wide door. Curious, she rounded the bed and moved to the threshold.

It was white and gold. The walls and floor were tiled with square slabs of what appeared to be marble. Stepping inside, Khalia saw that the fortress indeed boasted indoor plumbing, but she had never seen the like of this. Instead of a tub, the main feature of the room was a small, round pool that looked to be about eight feet in diameter. A half moon tiled wall surrounded one side. Spouts, gold, or at least gilded, protruded from the walls in a half dozen places, making Khalia wonder if they were spouts at all or served some other purpose she couldn't imagine. Peeking from a small alcove to one side was the rounded edge of what appeared to be the bowl of a porcelain throne. Along another short wall, a cabinet had been built to support a solid slab of marble nearly six feet long and about two feet wide. Centered in the slab was a washbasin filled by way of a golden faucet. There were no handles and Khalia wondered how the thing worked.

At Damien's touch, she jumped. He was frowning when she whipped her head around to look at him.

"I do not see how this garment fastens."

Khalia blinked at him. "Excuse me?"

"I am not familiar with this type of garment. How does one remove it?"

Khalia stared at him, dumbfounded, for several moments. Finally, dimly, it sank in. He'd offered to attend her--she was supposed to be royalty. "One doesn't," she said flatly. "One leaves while I attend myself."

His brows rose almost to his hairline but after a moment, he merely bowed and left. When the doors had closed behind him, Khalia removed what was left of her clothing. In truth, there wasn't much. She'd shredded it when she'd shifted and the tattered remains had been slowly disintegrating since.

She had no idea what she was going to wear when she finished bathing, but for the moment she was far more interested in getting clean. Sand showered down around her as she undressed and it occurred to her that there was so much dirt in her hair she was more likely to make mud than get clean unless she managed to get most of it sloughed from her skin and shaken from her hair before she got in. Removing the last of the pins that had held her hair coiled sedately on her head, she bent over at the waist and shook her hair out, combing as much sand from it as possible.

She stood for some moments in front of the pool, her hands on her hips, her gaze wandering around the tub, the walls, the lip of the tub. There were no handles. None. No levers. How was she supposed to turn the thing on?

She wasn't about to call Damien in to show her. It was bad enough that she'd had to parade around in front of him, and a dozen other men, filthy and half naked. She hadn't even seen a towel she could wrap up in. She supposed they must be kept in the cabinet beneath the lavatory, but she wasn't any more comfortable about the idea of asking him in wrapped in a towel, particularly considering the fact that every male she'd met so far looked at her as if he was starving and she a particularly tasty looking piece of food. And Damien *had* warned her that his self-restraint had its limits. After a moment, she decided to step into the strange thing and see if one of the 'spouts' was actually some sort of lever or knob.

She'd reached the center of the pool when she was abruptly deluged with water from every direction. Her shriek was instinctive and more from surprise than anything else.

"Highness?"

Khalia whirled so fast she slipped and sprawled in the tub, her legs splayed in front of her. She wasn't certain whether the water cushioned her fall and kept her from driving her spine through the top of her skull when she landed, or if she was just too shocked to feel the pain. After a moment, she managed to blink the water out of her eyes and gape at Damien.

He was staring at her like a starving man who'd just been offered a smorgasbord, his gaze riveted to the curling red thatch between her splayed thighs.

Recovering from her shock, Khalia slapped her legs together, then drew them up to her chest. Pointing a shaking finger toward the door, she said in a trembling voice, "OUT!"

The order seemed to break the spell, either that, or the fact that she'd managed to cover most of herself with her bent legs. He blinked at her, like a sleepwalker awakening. Finally, with great dignity, he bowed, turned on his heel and once again left her.

Khalia glared at the door as it closed behind him.

"You screamed, your highness. It is my duty to protect you from all threat."

Khalia's eyes narrowed. "There's not a single damned window in this bath!" she yelled in a very unladylike manner. "Exactly what did you think was threatening me?"

He was silent for several moments. Finally, with a hint of amusement tingeing his voice, he responded, "I am only a soldier, your highness. I am paid to act, not think."

General Damien Bloodragon, the King's Champion--not paid to think? Obviously, he thought he was dealing with an empty headed female. "If he pops through that door again, I'm going to find something and beat him severely about the head and shoulders," she muttered.

"Would you care to dine before you retire, your highness?"

Khalia climbed gingerly to her feet, rubbing her abused posterior. Instantly, the water, which had ceased to flow the moment she settled on the bottom of the tub, pelted her from every direction again. She clapped a hand to her mouth, stifling another yelp. When she was more certain of her footing, she slung the wet hair from her eyes.

She was tempted to just tell him to go to hell, but the truth was she hadn't had her dinner and she was starving. "Yes … thank you," she said finally.

She was fairly certain she didn't really care to be pelted with water from every direction, but she couldn't figure out any way to turn it off anymore than she'd been able to figure out how to turn it on to begin with. Once she'd found soap to lather her hair and body with, she revised her opinion. The spraying water quickly and efficiently removed the soap, a feat far more difficult when bathing in a tub. Strangely enough, the heated, pelting water also soothed her aching muscles.

She wasn't certain how long she stood mindlessly beneath the water, almost drowsing as it pummeled her aching body, but after a time it occurred to her that Damien had gone to prepare a meal for her.

She was alone.

She could escape.

She almost leapt from the shower as that thought occurred to her. Moving to the rim, she sat down long enough to wring the water from her hair and then climbed out and moved as quickly as she dared to the lavatory. It was then that she discovered it wasn't a cabinet beneath it as she'd supposed--not that she could tell at any rate. After feeling along it frantically for several moments, she finally decided it wasn't really that important. It would have been nice, but she would certainly dry, with or without a towel.

Clothes was the problem. Her own were beyond filthy and nothing but tatters anyway. Not that she would've minded a little dirt if it meant the difference between escaping and staying in this strange world, but she was really reluctant to run around naked. She didn't believe for one moment that Damien, or any of the dragon men, for that matter, could tell that she was nearing the end of her reproductive cycle, but they hardly needed that sort of incentive to attack her if she was flaunting herself.

Deciding finally that a sheet or coverlet was just going to have suffice, she headed for the door. She simply stared at the panels for several moments, wondering how she was supposed to make it open. There was no handle and no knob. As she moved toward it with the intention of pushing against it, however, the doors swung open, this time into the bedroom. Wasting no more time, Khalia snatched the coverlet from the bed, flung it around her shoulders and dashed into the sitting room.

There, she skidded to a halt.

Damien was standing near a table in one corner having just, apparently, set a tray down. She gaped at him.

His eyes narrowed. His gaze flickered over the bedspread she had draped around her like a roman toga.

She pasted a smile on her lips. "I couldn't find a towel."

One dark brow rose in a skeptical arch. He took a step toward her. Khalia's mind screamed 'run', but her feet remained firmly glued to the floor.

Chapter Four

Khalia's gaze, chained to Damien's by her awareness of guilt and fear of reprisal, tilted as he approached and towered over her. His face was expressionless, but his eyes were dark and tumultuous with comprehension, desire, irritation. She was left with no doubt at all that he'd immediately, and correctly, assessed the situation and he wasn't at all pleased about it.

Beyond the anger, however, heated desire, held barely in check, roiled inside of him. It was almost as fascinating and alluring as it was frightening.

Maybe it was *more* fascinating and alluring than it was frightening.

She wasn't accustomed to having men look at her as if they wanted to consume her. There was no getting around the fact that it was definitely unnerving. On the other hand, his simmering, barely controlled desire was enough to jump start her own with no more than a look.

She jumped when he grasped her shoulders, hoping--fearing--that she had unleashed the beast he was working so hard to tame. Her mouth went dry with anticipation. Warmth saturated her with liquid heat.

Abruptly, he spun her on her heels and nudged her toward the bedroom. Stunned, she didn't even think to protest as he guided her into the bedroom and to the small bench set before the vanity. When he'd pushed her down onto the seat, he took a comb from the table before her, lifted the hair that fell to her hips and, starting at the ends, began to carefully work the tangles from it. Khalia stared wide eyed at his reflection in the mirror, hardly daring to breathe.

"When you assume the throne … when you arrive in Caracaren, the principle seat of your domain, you will be given handmaidens to attend you, your highness. This is considered an honor and you may choose any of the maidens of the noble houses to wait upon you."

The deep, resonant timber of his voice was almost as soothing as his hands. He was a conundrum. As pleasing as he was to the eye, one had only to look at him to know that he was a fierce warrior and would be a deadly adversary on any field. She had seen it for herself, watched him dispatch three beast men within a very short space of time and leave the field without so much as a scratch. It was far easier to picture him with a sword in his hand than a comb, and yet he was surprisingly adept and gentle for someone who made his living by the sword. His dark hair was long, falling well past his shoulders, so perhaps that was why he knew that one had to start at the ends and work upwards rather than vice versa to untangle long hair, but it was just as easy to believe he had learned it in the boudoirs of many women.

The possibility disturbed her. It indicated an intimacy that went beyond slaking raw animal need.

She didn't want to think about the likelihood of a wife and children somewhere and she didn't want to consider why that bothered her.

She cleared her throat with an effort. "You are so certain they will welcome me?"

He paused in his task and his gaze met hers in the mirror. "You are the image of your mother. Even without the Tear no one would question your hereditary right to the throne of Atar."

Khalia's heart skipped a beat and her gaze moved from his to study the face that had been her mother's. For so many years she had wondered what her mother had looked like and now she found she had looked at her mother's face each time she looked into the mirror. "Truly?"

He paused in his task. Moving closer, so close she could feel the heat of his body, feel the light brush of his skin against her back, he reached around her and skimmed an index finger over the hollow in one cheek beneath her high cheek bone. "Her face was rounder here." He circled her rounded chin. "Her chin not quite so stubborn." His finger shook slightly as he traced the curve of her lips. Swallowing convulsively, he removed his hand. "Your mouth is … not the same, nor your hair."

After a moment, he ran the comb through her hair again, then lifted a thick lock, sifting it through his fingers. "Your hair is like … flame. I have never seen the like of it, nor anyone in all of Atar. This is your father's gift to you."

Oddly enough, she hadn't spent nearly as much time wondering about her father as she had her mother. She supposed that was because, in the back of her mind, she had wanted to blame someone besides her mother for abandoning her to the life of an orphan. She forced a faint smile. "I'd always wondered who to blame for it," she said in an attempt at lightness.

He frowned. "You did not know him?"

She shrugged off-handedly, as if it didn't matter. The truth was, it did. "I expect he was some mad Scotsman, or perhaps an Irish ruffian."

"But you carry the name of your sire?"

Khalia shivered slightly, despite the fact that the temperature of the air was perfectly comfortable, and pulled the bedspread more snugly around her shoulders. "I haven't a clue. The orphanage gave me my name, I expect. What was my mother's maiden name?"

"Emberhorn." Damien moved away from her to a paneled wall--or what appeared to be one until he reached it and the panel slid back into a recess, exposing a wall filled to overflowing with brightly colored fabrics. Khalia turned on the bench to watch him as he rifled through them, searching, she supposed, for garments. He'd said this was the royal apartments, but he'd also said the royals had not been here since her grandfather's time--whenever that was. Surely, even if he did find women's garments, they would be too aged to wear, out dated even if they fit--which seemed extremely doubtful.

After a moment, he pulled a long piece of … tissue from the armoire and held it up, examining it with a thoughtful frown. She could see him clearly through it. She felt certain she could've read a newspaper through it.

"You will wish to retire once you have eaten. Is this satisfactory?"

Khalia gave him a look. "I'm not certain. What is it for?"

He glanced up at that. "It is a sleeping garment."

She stared at him speechlessly. "You think I'm going to stroll around this--suite wearing nothing but that?"

He frowned. "You can not wear the bed linens. You are a princess of the house of Emberhorn."

Khalia pursed her lips. "Does everyone in this … world run around naked or nearly naked?"

"Your body is flawless. Why would you wish to cover it?" he asked curiously.

The remark was flattering and horrifying at the same time. If she'd had any doubt that he hadn't taken the opportunity to examine her thoroughly, he'd disabused her of the notion. She couldn't help but be pleased that he seemed to think she was beautiful, but all the same…. "For the sake of modesty? Decency?" she suggested.

And then there was the other thing, the fact that flaunting her naked body must seem like an open invitation to any randy male that happened along. It would seem almost as if she were saying, 'yes, you may look, but this isn't on tonight's menu'. And of course, being the perfect gentlemen they were they wouldn't throw her down and take what she hadn't intended to offer.

He frowned. "The customs are different where you came from."

That was an understatement if she'd ever heard one.

Returning, he helped her to her feet, pried the edges of the coverlet from her fingers and tossed the 'veil' over her head. It had been fashioned much like a poncho and in truth was no more than a length of cloth with a hole large enough for her head to fit through. Lifting her arms, he quickly tied two sets of ties on either side, one at breast level, the other around her hips … as if she was a small child and had no notion of how to dress herself. He was frowning as he tied the two halves of the gown together, but she wasn't certain whether it was from concentration, irritation, or her reluctance to wear the thing. "You must become accustomed to the ways of your people. We are dragon folk. The clothing we wear has nothing to do with a weak morality or a lack of modesty. We could not shift without destroying our garments if we were to swath ourselves from head to toe as you were when you arrived."

She honestly hadn't thought of that and, oddly enough, now that he had pointed it out, she began to feel a bit like a zealot. All the same, and despite the fact that he made a strenuous attempt not to ogle her, she felt distinctly uncomfortable and had to fight the urge to cover herself with her hands. She refrained only because she had no desire to draw his attention to those particular spots when he was ignoring them so assiduously. "What about the … uh … armor?"

Lifting her hand, he placed it on his arm and escorted her from the room into the sitting area. He pulled out a chair and held it for her while she sat. "It expands … to a degree. We can not wear full armor, but I have no need of it when I shift."

The tray, she saw with a good deal of surprise, held a large fowl and several side dishes. She knew she hadn't been in the bath long enough to prepare such a meal--at least not with the sort of kitchen facilities she was accustomed to. She had seen a number of marvels already, however. Or had he commandeered the meal of the royal guard, she wondered?

When he didn't take the seat across from her, she looked up at him. "You're not dining with me?"

"I will serve you."

Khalia blinked at him. "I will choke on my food if you stand over me."

Amusement gleamed in his eyes. After a moment, he moved to the chair across from her and sat down. The amusement vanished when she served the plates, but she ignored his look of disapproval.

"You must learn the ways of your people."

She frowned. She didn't want to learn the ways of 'her' people. She wanted to go home. "Tell me about my mother."

He studied her for a long moment, but finally turned his attention to the meal. "In truth, I know little. Those were … tumultuous times and I was no more than a captain when I was selected for the royal guard, but I did not guard the Queen's household. I was too … proud of my manhood to submit to gelding. It weakens a man, for, once gelded, he can not shift."

Khalia choked on the bite of chicken she'd just taken. It took her several minutes to catch her breath. Damien, she saw once she managed to dislodge the piece and drag in a decent breath, was on his feet and nearly as white faced as she was red. "I beg your pardon?" she said weakly.

He looked at her blankly, obviously having entirely lost his train of thought while she struggled for air. "You didn't guard the Queen's household...," she prompted, convinced that she must have heard him wrong.

He frowned, apparently mentally reviewing the conversation. When his gaze met hers once more, there was amusement in his eyes. "It has been practiced for eons--In order to protect the royal lines the guards must be gelded. It is neither permanent, nor, I've been told, painful."

"Oh. Then it's not ... what I thought it was."

His lips twitched. "I expect it is much like you thought it was. It is to prevent any chance of an undesirable breeding upon a royal." After a moment, however, he sobered. "Caracus was a powerful dragon, possibly the most powerful there had ever been. He bred three daughters upon his queen, securing his line ... but it cost him his queen and, in the end, his life."

The tale created far more questions in her mind than it answered. She'd been reared by strangers, among strangers, and yet she'd had grandparents, aunts ... possibly cousins.... Or maybe not. Maybe all had died, or been slain before she was even born?

As intriguing as she found the personal history of what he, at least, supposed to have been her family, the rest of his comments were almost as puzzling. "He ... Caracus had no male heir? Is that what caused the war?"

Damien looked at her curiously. "He had *three* female heirs. No king in living memory had born three. His own sire failed to produce a single female. He bore only males, which is what tore the kingdom apart."

Khalia merely stared at him. She was having a great deal of trouble getting her mind around the implications. "The monarchy is passed through the female line? This is ... a matriarchal society?"

He gave her a strange look. "Naturally."

Naturally? Khalia was so stunned she couldn't even think of how to respond to the remark.

"The female bears her young. There can be absolutely no doubt that her offspring is hers.... A bull will not stray from his female once they have mated, but he can not always prevent others from usurping his place. Occasionally, although it is rare, the female will not be satisfied with the male she had chosen and seek another, or even take a lover. In any case, it is in the nature of the female to promote society, peace and prosperity ... all things necessary to a good ruler. The male is stronger, aggressive and territorial by nature, far better suited to the protection of the realm from its enemies."

The food was good, and Khalia was hungry, but she found she was far more interested in assuaging her curiosity than her appetite. "So ... Caracus inherited the throne from his mother ... and insured his line by producing three female heirs? What happened to my mother? Why was there a war? I assume there was war?"

Damien pushed his plate away and sat back. "Caracus was crowned because he was the eldest offspring and there were no females. His brother, Houlin, stole Carcacus' queen in order to wrest the realm from his older brother. Caracus tore the kingdom apart searching for her. Those loyal to the King sent the princesses to safety through the portal. They didn't dare leave it open, however, so they gave each of the princesses a Tear--the amulet you wear. The amulet was designed to summon them home once peace had been restored. Unfortunately, we discovered that it did not work as we'd thought it would. We could not summon them home. We could only wait for them to use the Tear to return. And since the princesses did not know that they could not be summoned, or how to use the Tear to return...."

He paused, frowning. Finally, he rose and began to pace. "Caracus' beloved queen took her life to prevent Houlin from claiming her. When Caracus learned of it, he could not be restrained or reasoned with. War gripped the land until both Caracus and Houlin were slain in battle.

"When we realized we could not summon our princesses home, we were forced to place the youngest of the Gildwing offspring, Maurkis, on the throne as regent until such time as the true heir returned. There was something else we did not count upon, however, when we sent the princesses to the other world."

"Maurkis would resist giving up the throne to the heir, even if she showed up?" Khalia guessed.

Damien stared at her a long moment, but slowly shook his head. "He has given us no reason to believe he would not welcome the true heir." He frowned thoughtfully, but finally seemed to dismiss it. "That world we sent them to drains their life force. Princess Cassiamia, who should have been next in line after her father, returned, but she was aged. In less that ten of our years, she had grown ancient, weak in body, mind and spirit. She was not fit to rule. We thought, once she was home once more, that she might recover. She did not. We realized then that our only hope was that the offspring of one of our princesses would return to take the throne, but, in truth, we had almost given up hope of it … until we were alerted by the tear that you had passed through the portal."

He ceased pacing and turned to study her for a long moment. "Your people need you. I can not allow you to return to that world you have always believed to be your own. This is your world. It is your duty--to your people-- and to your family line, to assume the throne of Atar."

Chapter Five

It was just as well that Khalia hadn't really expected to rest, she thought wryly when she woke the following day. She couldn't ascribe her restless night to physical discomfort with her surroundings. The temperature of the quarters where Damien had imprisoned her was constant and so finely attuned to her comfort that she couldn't help but wonder if these beings had discovered a way to regulate such things--as farfetched as that seemed on the surface.

The bed was also comfortable.

It was her own body she was uncomfortable with. She was sensible enough to realize that giving the appearance of malleability was probably the safest thing she could do in her current circumstances. She was cool headed enough to present the facade of doing so, but the customs here boggled her conservative mind. Inside, she cringed at being the next thing to naked--around a man, no less. More than that, it made her aware of her own sexuality in a way she never had been, nor had ever particularly wished to be.

She was entirely certain that she would've been uncomfortable if she'd been completely alone. Damien Bloodragon magnified her awareness to such a degree that she had felt unnerved, jittery, and fragile even after he'd left her, at last, to herself. The most shockingly indecent dreams had plagued her throughout the night. As much as she'd always prided herself on her imagination, she couldn't even begin to guess where the images had come from.

Naturally, she wasn't a complete innocent. She was an educated woman. She had a working knowledge of the mechanics of human copulation even though she hadn't actually experimented with it. She wasn't even completely ignorant of the mating ritual that led up to it. She'd been kissed before--several times. The first time, she'd actually encouraged her beau to do so. It had even been rather pleasant to begin with. In the end it had been a disappointment, however, and she'd certainly not felt any great need to repeat the experiment. Others had tried, but after she'd soundly boxed their ears they'd learned to control their baser instincts around her.

She had dreamed of far more than a few chaste kisses, however! In fact, they hadn't been chaste at all, but rather downright carnal. She should have been as shocked and disgusted with the dream as she had been when her beau had stuck his tongue down her throat. Instead, in her dreams, she had *welcomed* his kisses--encouraged him!

She'd dreamed of his hands, too. She was fairly certain that part, at least, had been brought on by the way he'd stroked her face, although, to be honest with herself, just looking at those big hands of his made her heart flutter--except it wasn't her face he was stroking in her dreams.

She had an uncomfortable suspicion that she was going to have a hard time looking him in the eye the next time she saw him.

Frowning at the thought, she rose from the bed and went into the bath to perform her morning ritual. When she'd finished, she studied the pile of rags she'd discarded the night before and finally decided to wash them. Perhaps she could get a needle and thread and mend it? The clothing was ruined of course, and she doubted a magical seamstress could mend it in a way that would make it at all presentable, but it at least covered her nakedness.

When she emerged sometime later, she felt marginally better and crossed the room to the wall Damien had opened the night before, deciding she would see if she could discover something she might wear that didn't leave her feeling so exposed, so … wanton.

After all that had happened, she supposed she shouldn't have been surprised when the wall merely slid soundlessly open as she stopped before it, but she was. Immediately distracted from her goal, she stepped away. The panel slid closed.

Maybe, she decided, there was some sort of latch on the floor? A weight and pulley system? She felt around with her foot, but noticed nothing through the thick carpet. Finally, she got down on her hands and knees, pressing a palm into the carpet in search of a depression or lump that might support her theory.

"Lose something?"

Khalia's head snapped up of its on volition, twisting toward his voice so quickly a bone cracked in her neck. Damien was standing in the doorway, staring at her fixedly. His gaze wasn't riveted to her face, however. Resisting the urge to cover her posterior with her hand, Khalia scrambled to her feet. "What? Oh. No … uh.…" She found that she was very reluctant to tell him she'd never seen doors like those here and that she'd been trying to figure out how it worked. Pride might goeth before a fall, but she hated admitting complete ignorance about anything. "I was just curious about the fiber the carpet was made of. It doesn't really feel like cotton … or wool either."

His brows rose, but he apparently decided not to comment on her strange behavior. "Shall I assist you?"

"Assist me?" Khalia asked weakly.

He nodded toward the panel.

"Oh. No. I believe I can manage … thank you."

"I have brought your breakfast," he said. Bowing, he turned and left.

Khalia's shoulders slumped. Turning, she activated the panel and stood staring at the wardrobe for several moments before she began digging for something to wear. A half hour later she accepted the futility of finding anything she felt remotely comfortable about and simply dragged out a couple of pieces of teal colored, gauzy fabric and tossed them onto the bed. Either everything in the armoire was night wear, or this was as much as any of them ever wore.

The outfit she'd chosen wasn't quite as sheer as the 'nightgown' Damien had chosen for her to sleep in, but it didn't miss it by much. Holding them up, she examined the two pieces. One looked rather a lot like a veil, or perhaps a kerchief for her hair. The other looked a good bit like the 'gown' she was wearing except that it had a drawstring at one end and no other ties. It was also considerably shorter than the gown she was wearing which 'modestly' brushed her ankles.

It was unfortunate that she hadn't seen a female since she'd arrived. It would've been a good deal easier to figure these things out if she had. Shrugging, she tossed the gown off and pulled the 'dress' over her head. It was only open on one side, which seemed really odd. Was she supposed to wear it like a cape, she wondered? Or tie it on one side?

Finally, she shifted it around until she had one arm free of the fabric and picked up the matching piece. It, too, had a drawstring at one end. It was a very short drawstring, however, too short to tie it under her chin. Finally, she simply tied it in a bow and set it on top of her head like a coronet, with the veil hanging over her hair. She was still trying to figure out what to do with the two ties on the sides when Damien, apparently having decided she had taken too long, entered the room once more.

The look on his face made her want to hit him.

With an obviously strenuous effort, he curbed his amusement and strode toward her. Without a word, he untied the drawstring at her shoulder, pulled the 'cape' off and wrapped the skirt around her waist, tying it at one side. Khalia blushed to the roots of her hair, so mortified tears stung her eyes as he moved around behind her. Removing the 'veil', he gathered her hair and draped it over one shoulder, then placed the top over her breasts, tying the short tie around her neck. He then took the ties she hadn't been able to figure out what to do with and tied them in back, just below her shoulder blades. Stepping away from her, he dug in the armoire and returned with something that looked a lot like the thing he wore over his genitals, except that it was a wedge in the front, rather than bag-like. Kneeling, he stretched the thing out, waiting. After a moment, Khalia, dying of embarrassment, placed her hands on his shoulders and stepped into the thing, closing her eyes tightly as he pulled it up and adjusted it.

When he'd finished, she drew a shuddering breath and stepped away from him. He caught her arm when she would've left the room. She resisted, but she didn't want to get into a tussle and yielded readily enough, though reluctantly, when his grip tightened. He moved closer. Tucking an index finger beneath her chin, he forced her to look up at him.

The tears gathered in her eyes made it impossible to read his expression, not that she wanted to. She lifted her chin another notch to avoid his touch. He frowned, touching the tiny bead of moisture on one cheek. "What is this?"

She flushed, though not so heatedly as before. Instead of answering, she glared at him. "Don't taunt me. Isn't it enough that you embarrassed me?"

If she'd slapped him, she didn't think he could've looked more surprised or taken aback. "It wasn't my intention to do either, princess," he said gruffly.

She wasn't certain she believed him. On the other hand, the words had no sooner left her mouth than it occurred to her that she'd embarrassed herself. By not being able to figure out how the garments were supposed to be worn, she'd made herself look foolish. She sighed. Her menses, she decided, must be imminent for her to be so sensitive as to blow the situation all out of proportion. Ordinarily, she would probably have laughed herself. She would've still been embarrassed, but she would've been able to see the humor in it.

Shaking her head dismissively, she went into the living area of the suite. She wasn't particularly hungry, but she hadn't eaten much the night before. She couldn't allow her nerves to put her into such a state that she would grow weak and listless with the lack of food. She knew from personal experience that she would, and more nervous besides.

"How long will we stay here?" she asked when she'd settled in her chair.

"That depends."

"On what?"

"You."

Color climbed her cheeks, but she wasn't about to try to reason with him. Apparently the females in his world *did* come in season. She was naturally curious about it, but she rather thought she preferred the idea of consulting another woman for the information.

She considered it as she ate, wondering what might bring about such a development. A long gestation? It was hard to believe they might gestate longer than a human pregnancy when *that* took most of a year.

Their life span? He'd said that Princess Cassiamia had aged tremendously in her world. That was curious enough in itself, but she was more interested at the moment in figuring out the reproductive habits of these dragon folk.

Perhaps their life span was longer than the human life span and the female reproductive cycles were different because of it?

It made sense. Khalia was almost envious to think of not having to worry about her menses every month. Almost.

There *was* the little matter of having males fighting over who was going to mate with them when they *were* in season. That was downright scary.

She cleared her throat on that thought. "I suppose that means I must stay here … in the suite?"

Damien looked away uncomfortably. "I ordered the guard to secure a perimeter beyond the fortress. Under the circumstances, I thought it … best. The main danger at the moment is the possibility that their urges might overcome their training."

Khalia turned red. She did *wish* he'd stop referring to her in terms of breeding! From what she'd been able to tell, he seemed to having nearly as much difficulty thinking of something else as the men he'd accused. "Then it would be all right for me to look around the fortress?"

He seemed almost to shrug. "I will escort you."

She hadn't really expected him to allow her to go alone, but she wasn't particularly happy about it. On the other hand, the place had seemed huge. Maybe it would turn out to be for the best if she became familiar with it first? Perhaps, in a day or two, he would become less suspicious of her, or at least bored, and allow her to wander around alone?

Apparently, Damien decided to use the opportunity to improve her education. While they walked, he told her what he knew of her 'family' history, explained the workings of court, and Atar's class system. Khalia found it interesting, although she didn't consider it particularly useful information. She wasn't planning on staying.

On the other hand, the conversation was far more stimulating than the tour. The entire floor consisted of suites for the royal family and their entourage, and, for the first time, she discovered that Damien had placed her in her own mother's suite.

Apparently, the King, the Queen and each of the royal princesses had had their own separate apartments. On the floor below were more of the same, only for slightly less important people. On the level below that were 'business' rooms, the various offices and meeting rooms where governing of the realm took place when the royal family was in residence. The ground floor consisted of salons and bedchambers--no suites for those low born enough to lay their heads here.

There was also no entrance or exit that Khalia could see. She would've liked to have asked Damien about it, but she saw little sense in drawing his attention to her eagerness to be gone.

As they started back up, Khalia reluctantly set her agenda aside and cast about in her mind for a question that would make it seem as if she'd been giving her full attention to the lesson, which she hadn't. She'd been a little too preoccupied with trying to formulate plans of escape to listen except when he used a word that caught her attention. "That thingy you were wearing when I first met you … the head dress … what does it mean? Is it … it isn't like the head of your enemy or something like that?"

Damien gave her a look that left her in no doubt that she'd gravely insulted him. "We are not barbarians," he responded stiffly.

Khalia blushed. "I'm sorry. I didn't mean to be insulting."

He said nothing for several moments and she was beginning to think she'd so insulted him that he wouldn't speak at all. Finally, he smiled wryly. "It is a symbol of great honor, but in truth, an archaic one. In ancient times, very likely it *was* the head of an enemy."

"Honor? Because you are the King's champion? His highest general?"

He shook his head. "No. It means I am of pure blood, pure dragon, untainted with the blood of other tribes that inhabit our world. It is a rarity now."

Khalia felt insulted, although she wasn't entirely certain why. Part of it, she knew, was the remark he'd made about her being a half breed, but she couldn't figure out why she should care. The truth was, she didn't really believe she had *any* dragon blood, whatever he thought.

She supposed it might be because she didn't have the sense of connection people like him did with their forefathers because she wasn't even certain of who her parents were, much less theirs. There was also the barely acknowledged fear that her antecedents might be worse than merely poor. For all she knew her mother might have been a common whore, her father a thief, murderer, or rapist.

She told herself it was probably just as well she didn't know, might even be for the best if her fears were true, but she would've liked to know she had no reason to be ashamed of her roots.

"Only those of purest blood retain all the abilities of the old ones. The others are like those who tried to claim you-- they can not fully shift."

They had arrived, finally, at the door of her suite. As they entered, she turned to him, blocking his entrance into the suite. "Like me, you mean?" she said, trying to keep her voice carefully neutral.

His brows rose. "You are a female."

"I figured that out a long time ago. I had the distinct feeling you'd figured it out a while back, too."

His lips tightened at her sarcasm. "Females lost the ability to fully shift long ago, before memory."

Khalia gaped at him. "So … you're saying they're absolutely defenseless against these great brutes?"

His eyes narrowed. "They have their tongues … and yours seems sharp enough."

Khalia narrowed her eyes, as well. If she'd been tall enough, she would've been nose to nose with him. "I didn't get the impression that those … those beasts out there wanted to talk. Precisely what do you think I could've done with my sharp tongue to stop them?"

Something flickered in his eyes. At just about the same moment Damien grasped her upper arms and hauled her toward him it occurred to Khalia that her last remark hadn't come out exactly as she'd intended.

It also occurred to her that he'd been behaving like such a perfect gentleman that she'd forgotten a) that he'd previously shown every indication of a man on the edge, and b) he was by far the worst beast of all, the blue blood of dragons.

Chapter Six

"Were it not for my honor and my dedication to duty, I would sup from your lips and taste at last the essence that is driving me mad with need and there is only one word you might utter that could stop me," Damien growled in a low, husky whisper, his lips so near her own his heated breath caressed the sensitive surfaces, sending tingles of sensation through her that created its own heady wine.

Weak with the rush of chemical intoxicant, her anger completely forgotten, Khalia lifted her gaze with an effort to look up at him. For many long moments, their gazes locked. Her thoughts scattered, her instincts and desires warred for dominance, the tiny voices of caution and reason distant and failing to generate any sense of need for self preservation. She could stop him. She knew he still retained enough control that her denial would not fall on deaf ears.

She couldn't find the want inside herself to speak it and break the spell. The desire to fall more deeply into the unexplored chasm he tempted her with held sway over her mind and body.

Slowly, his face twisted with pain. He closed his eyes, resting his forehead against hers as he struggled with a ragged breath. "Say it, sheashona," he growled hoarsely. "On my honor, one taste would not be enough for me. I

fear … I *know* I could not stop. I would heed nothing …
not your pleas … not those of the gods themselves.

"Say it before we are both lost. Before Olgin no torture
any fertile mind could devise as my just reward for
dishonoring my queen could be worse than what I have
endured these past days."

Nothing short of a deluge of icy water could have more
surely or swiftly ripped her from the verge of total
capitulation. A tide of fear washed all before it. Khalia
shivered.

Before she could gather her scattered wits, however, he
drew slightly away from her, sliding his hands down her
arms until they encircled her wrists. Pushing her arms
behind her back, he manacled both wrists with one hand.
Very deliberately, he caught the edge of her top and
snapped the tie on one side, thrusting the cloth aside to
expose one heaving breast. Just as deliberately, he lowered
his head and caught her nipple in his mouth, sucking.

Khalia lost her breath as a jolt of knee weakening pleasure
went through her. She gasped, struggling against his hold,
arching her back in an effort to gain her release. He
clamped his lips more tightly over her breast, suckling
harder. The pleasure that shot through her was so intense a
wave of blackness followed behind it. "No," she said
faintly and not very convincingly even to her own ears.
Struggling to close her mind to the debilitating sensations
erupting through her, she moistened her lips and tried
again. "Damien, please stop."

For several horrifying moments, she thought he wouldn't
listen. He released her nipple at last, lifted his head slowly
and stared at her, breathing harshly. Finally, as if he had to
focus on his hands and mentally will them to release her,
his grip slowly relaxed. Drawing a deep, shuddering breath,
he stepped away from her, turned abruptly on his heels and
left.

The door closed behind him.

Khalia stared at the panels, shaking with reaction. Finally,
she moved to the nearest couch and sat, drawing her knees
up and hugging them to her.

She wasn't certain what had happened. One moment they had been snipping at each other, the next…. Heat washed through her at the memory. The muscles low in her belly clenched painfully. Her femininity ached. It didn't take prior experience or a great mind to understand why.

Her body yearned for his with a will of its own, without conscience, without any anxiety about consequences or morality. She had never been subject to the whim of instinct. She had believed, wrongly it seemed, that logic and intelligence always prevailed over primitive instinct.

She couldn't have been further from the truth, even as it applied to herself. From the moment he had pulled her tightly against him, morality had never entered her mind. Fear of the consequences to herself hadn't either. Nothing but her fear of the consequences to him had held any weight with her whatsoever … and she shuddered to think what her ignorance of the customs of this world might have cost him if he hadn't had enough sense to warn her.

In truth, ignorance wasn't just shameful. It could be deadly.

She had only been interested in the things he told her in a distant, clinical sort of way, as something she might want to catalogue for later study … when she was home again and beyond reach of the real meaning of any of it. She should have been more cautious. This world was far advanced from the one she'd left behind in many ways, and in others far more savage.

Remembering how she'd come to be here in the first place, she amended that to 'at least as savage'.

She wasn't entirely at fault, but ignorance wasn't an excuse. It would certainly give her no comfort if he was executed on her account, because she'd allowed her instincts and primitive urges to outweigh her common sense.

Despite those thoughts, she found it hard to accept, especially in light of his behavior toward her since she'd arrived. Perhaps, as her guard and mentor, he was allowed far more than one might expect ordinarily? Or, perhaps, he hadn't meant it literally?

She found it hard to believe that any civilization as advanced as this one seemed to be would behave in such a barbaric manner as to use torture on prisoners, for any reason, certainly not on someone who'd done no more than engage in consensual sex ... because it most certainly would have been consensual, not rape by any stretch of the imagination.

Of course, that might have been what he'd meant. He'd said he didn't think he could stop. Another wave of heat washed through her at the thought. It took an effort to ignore it, but she was as unnerved by what he'd said as she was by her reaction to him. She was no more certain, if it happened again, that she would have the strength to tell him no than he, apparently, was that he'd be able to stop.

It occurred to her after a moment that she was probably hampered by her knowledge of the customs considered acceptable in medieval Europe. Despite some notable similarities, there were probably far more differences than she could imagine.

He had plainly said this was a matriarchal society. The female line was followed, the queen ruled unless she had only a male heir. But what of the tendency to form alliances through marriage? Was that the same? Was that what he'd meant? The royals could only wed other royals from the ruling houses of this world?

The female held the right to decline, regardless of how savagely the males fought for her favor ... and the penalty was death by torture for any male that ignored it?

She was suddenly certain that that was what he'd meant. He'd said he didn't think he could stop, even if she demanded it. But it seemed to her that he had been trying to warn her that she could not accept him. Why? He was a noble, but not a royal? Or was it even more complicated than that?

If the males were mindless, rutting beasts when the females were in season, perhaps the females were little better off? Perhaps it was forbidden to choose a mate at a time when neither party was capable of thinking rationally?

It seemed probable, at least in the case of royalty and the upper classes. Perhaps those of the lower classes weren't subject to more than their instincts, but the upper classes would almost certainly have to consider issues beyond those that were personal.

She was in serious trouble, far worse than she'd realized to begin with.

If it was true that the females of this world came in season, then it would follow that that was not a common occurrence. Very likely longevity was a factor and it was a natural sort of birth control and selective breeding.

She might or might not have dragon blood, but there was no doubt at all that she was completely human when it came to her reproductive cycles. She was as regular as the moon--Earth's moon. Unless the passage had somehow changed her, or these people were scientifically advanced enough to manipulate nature, there was going to be hell to pay.

Flight no longer seemed merely a matter of her own survival, but quite possibly the survival of this realm. It didn't take a great deal of imagination to envision the place descending into a constant, savage battle over the one female who was almost constantly 'in season'.

Or they would have to imprison her in some deep, dark dungeon where she could do no harm.

Rising abruptly, she went into the bath and retrieved the sad remains of what had once been her best suit. It was still damp since she'd had to lay it across the lip of the pool to dry, but it was dry enough for repairs. When she'd returned to the living area, she dropped the suit on the couch cushion and began a search for a sewing basket.

She didn't expect to find mending supplies. It boggled the mind only to imagine a princess performing such a menial task and in any case the clothing the people of Atar wore could not require a great deal of mending--probably couldn't hold up to much mending. The apartment was filled with elaborate needlework creations, however. It seemed likely that the queen must have entertained herself with her needle a good deal of the time.

Despite her expectations, she was still surprised when she discovered one. Settling on the couch once more, she spent the rest of the evening carefully repairing the suit. There were pieces missing and she had to sacrifice a good bit of length in the skirt to replace them, but she realized that it was very fortunate she was no flapper. There was plenty of fabric to cut and still maintain some decency.

She was fairly certain Damien would not want to return to the suite again so soon after what had transpired between them, but she suspected duty would win out when it came time to feed her. Since she didn't want to alert him to her plans, she placed a half finished tapestry in her lap with the suit under it.

There was no black thread to match the suit. She hardly thought it mattered. The suit was ruined anyway, but she chose the nearest color she could find to black.

She was so engrossed in her task that she didn't actually register the fact that Damien had entered the room until the clatter of the tray hitting the table jerked her out of her abstraction. She looked up guiltily then, but discovered she needn't have worried. Damien left once more without once glancing in her direction.

She watched him until the door closed behind him, feeling a mixture of emotions she found hard to identify. She found she didn't really want to examine them. Setting her work aside, she flexed her cramped fingers and finally rose, stretching to relieve her stiff muscles.

It occurred to her as she sat down that she might need food and water. She was fairly confident that she could find her way back to the area where the tunnel lay. If nothing else, it seemed likely the carnage Damien had left in their wake was bound to attract scavengers who would mark the spot. They had flown, however, and she had no idea how long it might take to hike the distance.

After a quick mental calculation, she took the quantity of food she might reasonably be expected to consume and divided it in half. When she'd eaten half, she wrapped the remainder and found a cool, dark spot near the floor to hide it, then returned to her task.

Her internal clock told her it was very late before she was finally satisfied that she'd done all that could be done. Smoothing the suit, she took it into the bedroom and looked around. She could put it in the armoire, she supposed, but she rather thought that, despite the quantity of clothing inside, the black would contrast sharply enough to stick out. After a few moments, she folded the suit and tucked it under the edge of the mattress, then crawled into the bed as she was, pulled the covers up to her chin and, within moments, slept.

She discovered when she woke that her 'granny had come to visit'. For some unfathomable reason, that made her feel like weeping. The feminine products awaiting her in the bath surprised her, embarrassed her and finally threw her into a rage. By the time she'd called Damien every foul word she'd ever been privileged to hear, it dawned upon her that he hadn't lied or exaggerated when he'd claimed he knew she was ripe for breeding. Without a doubt, he had the ability to sense the subtle hormonal changes the finest doctors of her world couldn't detect with all of their science. And obviously, before she'd even known it herself, he had detected the end of her cycle.

It was beyond embarrassing.

When she'd bathed and wept herself dry, she dressed and went into the living room. There she found a breakfast tray awaited her.

She was tempted to pick the whole tray up and throw it across the room. Instead, she comported herself like the lady she had worked so hard to become. When she'd finished, she retired to the couch to entertain herself with her mother's needlework and her thoughts.

She couldn't understand why she felt so morose, or so tense and on edge. The moment she'd been awaiting had arrived. She hadn't really believed Damien. More accurately, maybe, she hadn't wanted to believe him, but she'd known she didn't have much chance of escaping if there was even the slimmest chance that what he said was true. Even if Damien didn't come after her, she would've had to worry about other male dragons finding her, but, if it *was* true, then this period in her cycle would be the safest to attempt a flight for freedom.

When Damien appeared with her luncheon and then left again, just as he had with her dinner the night before and her breakfast that morning, Khalia decided that she had as much freedom from observation as she was going to get.

When she'd finished her luncheon, she decided to try the door to the suite. To her relief, it opened to her command just as it had Damien's. After glancing up and down the corridor, she hurried down the hall toward the stairs and rushed down them. She had to stop for several moments when she reached the ground floor to catch her breath.

There had to be some way out of the fortress on this floor. Damien and the guards had flown in over the ramparts, but Damien had said the females didn't have the ability to fully shift. It was possible, of course, that they still had the ability of flight, but it seemed logical that supplies, at least, would be moved via the surface of their world in some sort of conveyance. The fortress was enormous. Fully occupied, it must hold hundreds, perhaps even thousands of people and that translated into a great deal of supplies.

Moving directly toward the outermost walls, Khalia searched, room by room, hall by hall. By the time she'd explored the circumference, she estimated that she'd been talking to walls for at least three hours. She hadn't seen anything that even remotely resembled a door. "Open" had opened a lot of doors, but none that led beyond the fortress.

Disheartened, she turned toward the stairs. She doubted Damien would bring her dinner for another hour at least, but she didn't want to chance being outside the room when he did arrive.

She discovered she'd misjudged the elapsed time. She was still panting for breath when the door opened and Damien stepped into the room with her dinner tray. Holding her breath, she stared at him wide eyed for several moments, ducking her head toward the needlework in her lap when she saw that he would glance her way.

Instead of leaving as he had each time before, he paused, studying her. Khalia thought she would pass out with the effort to regulate her heart rate and breathing. Finally, without a word, he turned and vanished through the door once more.

Khalia let out the breath she'd been holding and got to her feet shakily, wondering just how acute his senses were. Could he hear and smell things that no human could, like some of the beasts on her world? Or was his hypersensitive awareness limited to the reproductive process?

Despite all he'd told her and all she'd learned, she still knew very little about this world or the inhabitants of it.

He could not have known she was out searching the fortress for an escape route, however. Surely, if he had, he would have come in search of her ... unless he knew that flying was the only way out and she didn't have that ability?

She shook her head. She was allowing her imagination to run wild with her. If he suspected anything at all, it was because she'd behaved so guilty--stared at him and attracted his attention--been breathing so heavily he would've had to have been deaf not to notice.

He'd left, though, without commenting on it. How was she to take that? Would he be laying in wait for her the next time she ventured forth? Or had she been right to begin with? He wasn't worried because there was no way out.

She was exhausted, emotionally and physically and by the time she'd eaten, it took an effort to stay awake. She went into the bath and splashed cold water on her face. She didn't have time to pamper herself. Her courses never lasted more than a few days and that left a narrow enough window of opportunity as it was. She had to find a way out, fast, or she might lose any chance of returning to Earth.

Her reproductive situation aside, Damien was bound to think it would be safe to move her and was probably making arrangements even now.

When she decided she had waited long enough that Damien was probably settled in his own suite for the night, she went to the door and cautiously checked the corridor. To her relief it was empty. Hurrying now, she rushed to the stairs and down them once more. She paused when she reached the ground floor, wondering if she should try checking it one more time. Finally, she decided to check the basement level. It seemed doubtful that she would find anything, but it was possible that there was a subterranean entrance to the place, perhaps a tunnel leading through the mountain the fortress hugged.

The stairs ended at a corridor that led, she discovered, directly to the exit she'd been searching for.

Chapter Seven

Khalia was tired and she hadn't even found the end of the tunnel. It was just as well that she hadn't spared the time to explore the exit even a little before she'd returned to the suite and prepared to leave. She wasn't certain if she had that she would've been willing to face the prospect.

Instead, as soon as she'd found the exit, she'd hurried back upstairs, changed into her mended suit and gathered the food and water she'd hoarded for her trek. As nearly as she could tell, the tunnel was straight, and aligned due north--or, at least what she thought of as north. Who knew what was what on this strange world? The desert lay south of the fortress and thus the tunnel to her own world. It was a setback, particularly when she had no idea of how far out of her way this tunnel would lead her, but she'd found no other route.

She couldn't fly, and even if she was desperate enough to try to climb down the almost smooth outer wall from the ramparts, she doubted she would've been able to find rope to aid her in the climb. The basement and tunnel could be nothing but a service entrance. It was too poorly lit to be anything else. These lights functioned in the same way as most of the lights she'd seen since her arrival--they illuminated in the presence of a living being, or perhaps movements--and they went off again when that person left the area. In the tunnel, however, there was no broad illumination. Instead, single globes, widely spaced, lined the ceiling of the tunnel. Once she'd walked for a time, both ends lay in darkness, not just the one before her.

Shivering uneasily, Khalia increased her pace. She'd been walking for nearly an hour when she came upon a cavernous room. Although the illumination was somewhat better, the room was filled with shelves that were in turn filled with boxes and barrels of every size and shape, and the towering shelves cut off a good bit of light. She continued straight and discovered that, in roughly the center of the room, was a sort of cross road. Standing in the center, she could see at each end of the room a tunnel like the one she'd been following, these branching east and west.

Without debating the matter, she turned east, certain that it would take her somewhat closer to her destination than the west bound tunnel. She had not been following the east bound tunnel long when she heard a sound from behind her. Instantly, the hair along her nape prickled. She halted abruptly, whirling to look behind her. Blackness greeted her and another shiver traveled along her spine.

She'd almost decided her imagination was playing tricks on her when she heard another faint sound. "Damien?" she called shakily.

There was no answer. Instead, she saw a form moving through the darkness toward her. Her heart leapt into her throat. She was suddenly certain that it wasn't Damien.

Whirling, she raced down the tunnel. She had a head start on whoever it was. Moreover, the tunnel wasn't big enough for a shifter--she didn't think. It wasn't much of an advantage, but it was something.

The boots she'd borrowed had high heels and weren't designed for running. They weren't particularly comfortable for walking for that matter, but she'd arrived barefoot. She hadn't worn shoes since. It hadn't seemed to matter since she'd been confined to the fortress, primarily the suite, and the floors were carpeted. She hadn't wanted to be forced to walk barefoot through the desert, however.

Now, she was almost sorry she'd decided to wear the boots instead of carrying them. She thought she might have been able to run faster without them. On the other hand, the skirt of her suit restricted her movements, as well. She knew from the sounds behind her that whoever, or whatever, it was, it was gaining on her, but she didn't dare spare the time to look back to see how much.

She'd begun to despair of her chances of escaping it when, dimly, ahead of her, the lights illuminated a door. If it was an exit, and not simply a door to another room, or another corridor, she might have chance. It occurred to her, though, that if it was an outer door, it would almost certainly be locked for security. As she raced toward it, she frantically searched it with her gaze. There was no sign of a knob or lever and no sign of the sort of locks she was familiar with. It might open when she neared it and it might not. It was possible that, like the door to the suite, it required a voice to open it. She began yelling 'open' before she reached it. Nothing happened. "Princess Khalia! Open!" she yelled breathlessly.

The door remained stubbornly closed and she had a bad feeling it wasn't going to open when she reached it.

It didn't.

She slammed into it and bounced back. When she hit the floor, she spared a glance back at last to see what it was behind her and how imminent it was. The thing behind her was far more terrifying than a dragon. It had the barrel chest of a bull, but neither of the two heads protruding at the ends of the snake-like necks looked bull-like. One looked like some sort of prehistoric cat, the other vaguely resembled a dog. Both heads sported wide, slathering jaws full of long, spiky teeth.

Scrambling to her feet, Khalia launched herself at the door again, clawing at the edges while she babbled every combination of 'Open up, Damn it to Hell' that she could think of. It opened so abruptly, she sprawled outside. Someone, or something, grabbed her. She screamed, trying to fight it off.

It grunted, a sound of satisfaction rather than pain or exertion, as it lifted her off the ground, wrapping two huge, hairy arms around her. Mindless with fear by now and expecting that thing that had been behind her to land on both her and her captor any second, she clawed at the arms and finally reached behind her to claw at her captor's face. He released her abruptly, but before she'd managed to take three steps, he caught the cloth of her suit, jerking her to a halt. She twisted, trying to pull free, but a meaty fist connected with her head. The shock of terror prevented her from feeling a great deal of pain. Instead, like the distorted sound from beneath water, she heard a smacking, meaty sound, felt her head ricochet off of something immovable and then blackness welled around her as she recoiled backward and hit the ground again.

* * * *

Damien had been pacing the ramparts for hours, as he had nightly, and much of his days, as well, since he had been sent to meet the princess Khalia, daughter of Rheaia and take her to safety. He was all too aware of the source of most of his restlessness.

Unfortunately, Khalia was also.

It would have been easier to bear, he thought, if she found his touch distasteful.

He was likely to lose his head, literally, over her before this was done.

He was a noble and of superior blood lines, but his position was not elevated enough for him to be seriously considered by the council as a prospective mate for a royal. It seemed more than likely that any attempt to place himself on the list would be considered an act of aggression if not outright treason.

And yet he feared he could not remain by her side to protect her, knowing he would never be allowed anything more without losing all sense of honor--without losing all sense of self-preservation.

The fact that she was no longer fertile and therefore the danger of siring a child on her had passed should have brought him some ease. It hadn't. In truth, he hadn't been able to think much beyond the fact that he could slake his lust for her without the disastrous consequence of siring an unacceptable heir upon her royal highness, Princess Khalia. It meant that he could avoid the slow, painful death reserved for those guilty of highest treason. It meant that he might have her as his lover for a year without having to give her up to another.

It meant that he would be condemning himself to a life of watching his place usurped by another male once a consort was selected for her and he knew he would not be able to endure it.

Now, he was desperate enough to consider a year of joy worth a lifetime of agony, but he yet retained enough honor, and enough of a sense of self-preservation to resist the impulse. That resistance was failing fast, however, and he had begun to look forward to relinquishing sole responsibility for Princess Khalia as a possibility of deliverance.

He was not comfortable about abandoning her to learn her way around strangers, but in truth he was no fit mentor for her and little more than a stranger himself. It would be for the best, he was certain, for both of them. Once she was in her uncle's care, her days would be filled with learning the ways of government and the customs of her people. She must be prepared for coronation and begin to review those males deemed fit to rule beside her.

She was young yet, but she could not have more than four or five breeding seasons left and she would not be allowed long to settle on a consort.

If he had had even a remote tie to one of the royal houses, he might have been chosen for his skills as soldier and tactician. If her own line had not been despoiled by her mother's unfortunate choice as a human as mate, he might still have been considered.

He felt certain, however, that neither the people nor the council would consider it acceptable for a princess, whose own lines were corrupted, to wed a male who was merely a noble.

After a time, he shook those thoughts off. His blood had cooled--somewhat--enough at any rate that he could think more clearly, and he'd begun to realize that a part of his restlessness was the sense that something was not quite right.

When the Tear had alerted them that Khalia had passed through the barrier, there had been no time to lose, and none for any sort of concrete plans. The land where the portal lay was no longer a part of Atar, but held now by their enemies, the Baklen. It had been understood, however, that he would return at once with the princess. Under the circumstances, he had not been able to, nor had he had any way to send word explaining the delay until they had reached the fortress.

He had sent a man with word, however, as soon as he had the princess secured within the fortress.

The outpost he'd chosen was the closest to the portal, but it was a remote one and had not been used since King Caracus' time. Regardless, it was not so remote as to preclude sending an entourage for the future queen. For nearly a week, they had been holed up in the fortress. A contingent of soldiers should have arrived by now even if not the princess' household.

There were many possibilities to explain it and not all of them meant that there was a threat, but he'd begun to wonder if his messenger had gotten through at all--and why, if the messenger had not was there not an army currently crawling over the landscape in search of them?

Regent Maurkis, Princess Khalia's uncle, was a weak male far more interested in his pleasure than the needs of the realm, and not particularly clever, but even so it seemed his advisors would have taken action by now.

He had been debating for the past two days whether to try to send another messenger. They were dangerously undermanned as it was, however, and if a second messenger failed to return without a regiment, he would've given up two more men than he could afford to lose.

It had not been safe to try to move the princess before because of her condition and, since they had been forced to linger so long that her enemies almost certainly knew of her arrival and quite possibly her vulnerability, it was equally dangerous, or perhaps even more dangerous to try to move her now than it had been before.

He was so deep in thought that it was several moments before he noticed the call of the captain of the guard. He stopped abruptly when he finally noticed it, lifting his head. More loudly the mind call repeated and this time Damien heard it clearly.

The perimeter had been breached.

Damien ordered Captain Swiftwing to send three men to each of the access tunnels beneath the fortress and the remainder to meet him at the princess' suite. Even as he whirled to race inside, however, he realized the princess was either asleep or she was no longer in her suite. He could not sense so much as a whisper of her mind talk.

He raced to her suite anyway, searching it quickly before he returned to the corridor and cast about for her scent, for any trace of her mind.

His heart nearly stopped in his chest when he heard the faint, but unmistakable, echo of her screams. Resisting the urge to leap immediately into action, he expanded his dragon senses, searching until he determined her direction. Abruptly, he turned and retraced his steps to the ramparts. Leaping up onto the breast high wall, he dove from it, shifting as he plummeted toward the rocks below.

The princess is taken by the southern service corridor! To arms! To your princess!

His dragon vision and hearing allowed him to see them and hear them long before he was within reach of them. His helplessness was maddening, driving the last vestiges of his civilized self beyond his awareness.

* * * *

Khalia felt herself skidding over a rough, pebbled surface instead of bare ground. Fire erupted from her palms, knees and thigh as the skin was ground away by the abrasive surface. She gasped, feeling the blackness recede slightly. She was still groaning in pain when she was pulled to her feet.

Despite the moonlight, or perhaps because the shock of her attack had severely limited her perceptions, Khalia could see very little. She was grateful for it. The beast that had chased her, she saw, was no more than two yards from where she stood with her captor.

"We should kill her here and be gone," the beast growled from both mouths at once, producing a strange, echo-like sound.

"No. We'll take her across the border and hide her body there like we agreed."

When Khalia managed to twist around enough to see the creature that held her, she was sorry she hadn't lost consciousness. She'd thought the beast no more than that, but the one that held her was the same horrible sort of mutation. "We're wasting time. She might have been heard."

At that, she was lifted free of the ground as the creature holding her stood upright and began to trot briskly away. She hung limply from the arm that encircled her. As painful as the blow had been and the fall afterwards, the jostling hurt far worse. It was a struggle to breathe and her ribs felt as if they might crack from the pressure of his grip and her own weight, but she thought her only chance to escape them might be in convincing them that she was defenseless.

Which, in point of fact, she pretty much was.

The scenario of being accosted by two thugs with the intention of doing away with her was beginning to get old. She'd had some clue, though, of the Chicago thugs' motives. What motive might these two have?

She couldn't hazard a guess and she rather thought later would be a better time to wonder. As some of the shock wore off, the pain seemed to intensify, but her reasoning processes also kicked into gear. Remembering the abduction that had landed her here in the first place, she thought it possible shifting might give her an element of surprise. She was stronger and faster when she shifted, but she doubted even that would give her an edge over this pair. The sudden increase in mass might break the creature's hold on her, though, and if she was free, she might be able to outrun them.

She was struggling to concentrate when she realized it was rapidly growing dark. For a split second, she thought she might be losing consciousness, but she realized in the next moment that the crackling sound in her ears was the sound of wings. She looked up at about the same moment her captors did.

Both let out sounds such as Khalia had never heard in her life and began to run faster. They stopped abruptly as dragons hit the ground all around them. The arm around her middle tightened until she was struggling for air. A great, clawed hand seized her head and Khalia squeezed her eyes shut, expecting any moment to feel her neck snap.

"Release her, now, and I will give you a swift death," Damien Bloodragon growled in the low, rumbling voice of his dragon. "Harm her further and you will beg me for death before I grant it."

Chapter Eight

"You will kill us either way," the creature holding her growled.

"You have touched Princess Khalia. The penalty is death."

"Let us cross the border and we will release her."

"No."

"I could kill her now and die knowing I have defeated you," the creature holding her growled.

Damien moved closer. "You will die knowing that I will track down your mates and your offspring and kill them slowly."

The arm around Khalia loosened fractionally. He lowered her until her feet once more touched the ground. "You will give me your word of honor before I release her that you will not wipe out my line."

"Give me no reason to do so and you have it."

The hand was slowly withdrawn from her head and Khalia breathed a little easier. Abruptly, the creature snatched her off her feet again, lifted her above his head and tossed her as if she were no more than a small child. Khalia gasped a short scream. It was cut off abruptly as Damien caught her midair and pulled her close to his huge, scaly chest, holding her with surprising gentleness.

"Seize them. Find out who sent them," Damien growled above her head.

Khalia turned at the sound of a scuffle behind them, just in time to see the two creatures whip knives from the belts at their waists and slit their own throats. She gaped at them in disbelief and horror, too stunned to look away.

"Olgin's balls!" Damien roared in fury.

As if the oath had broken a spell, Khalia finally managed to force her gaze from the horrendous sight, burying her face against his chest. Damien's arms tightened around her.

"Captain Swiftwing … take the men and search the fortress for assassins. When you've secured the fortress, see if you can track these two. I want to know everything you can discover about them."

The captain saluted and turned to his men as Damien, with a flap of his great wings, launched himself into the air. Khalia felt her stomach go weightless and reached up to wrap her arms around Damien's neck. She discovered it was a useless effort. He was many times the size of his human form now.

"I will not drop you, sheashona," he said in a low, rumbling voice.

Khalia shook her head, but she didn't try to explain that it wasn't fear but rather a need for comforting that had made her reach for him. She wasn't even certain of where the impulse had come from … some primal instinct, she supposed, for she had grown to adulthood in an institution. She had never asked for, or been given, the comfort of an embrace purely for reassurance.

She felt weak all over now that the danger had passed. She discovered, once Damien had landed on the ramparts and set her on her feet, that it wasn't purely her imagination. Her knees wobbled and threatened to buckle the moment Damien released her.

Without a word, he scooped her into his arms once more and headed toward the entrance to the fortress, shifting almost mid-stride from dragon to man once more. Khalia was stunned by the sudden, seemingly effortless, transformation. Even when she concentrated for all she was worth she had difficulty shifting and as often as not failed to do it at all. Compared to others in what she'd considered her own world, she had felt like she had a rare and amazing gift. Here, she thought she was more a freak of nature than anything else. It wasn't much of a gift when it would neither free her nor save her.

When they reached the suite, Damien settled her on a couch and knelt before her. Hooking a finger under her chin, he pushed her face up and looked it over in frowning concentration. With utmost care, he probed the side of her face and head. Finally, he sat back, sighing gustily. "I can not detect any broken bones. Where else were you injured?"

Khalia shook her head. "Just scrapes and bruises." She was lucky, all things considered and she knew it. From out of no where the urge to burst into tears overwhelmed her. Uttering a choked sob, she threw her arms around his neck, buried her face against it and gave vent to the pain and fear.

Damien stiffened. For several moments, he seemed to debate whether to thrust her away or to simply allow her to do as she pleased. Finally, he lifted a hand and stroked her hair tentatively.

It occurred to Khalia after a few moments, that she was making him excruciatingly uncomfortable. With an effort, she tamped the flow and slowly pulled away from him, searching frantically for a handkerchief.

The suit she'd spent so many hours mending was filthy and ripped once more. That in itself was almost enough to set her off again. Instead, she drew in a deep shuddering breath, tore a piece off to use for a handkerchief and mopped her face and nose.

Damien was staring at her, a troubled look on his face. "What is this?" he asked, touching the tears that still streamed down her face.

Khalia shrugged, sucked her trembling lower lip a moment and finally drew in another calming breath. "I'm sorry. I don't know what came over me. I never cry."

A hint of amusement entered his eyes. "This is cry?"

The comment sent such a wave of surprise through her that Khalia felt the last vestiges of her tears vanish. "You don't know what crying is," she said, stunned. Until that moment, she hadn't realized how different she was from the beings here. She knew it wasn't that they felt no emotion, but they undoubtedly expressed it, or released it, differently. Perhaps they had no tear ducts? But then, why was the amulet called the tear if they didn't even know what tears were?

He shook his head. "I have not seen this before. What is the purpose of it?"

Khalia was suddenly embarrassed. Wrapping her arms around herself, she drew her knees up on the couch, curling into a tight ball. "To express emotions too painful to keep inside; pain, fear, sorrow," she said uncomfortably. "It's a sort of release."

His brows rose, then descended again. "To help heal wounds?"

Khalia looked at him wryly. Supposedly, they helped to heal wounds to the soul, but somehow she doubted he would understand that. She shrugged.

He took it as a yes. Rising, he looked down at her a long moment. "You must seek your beast to aid your healing. I will prepare a bath for you and then we must talk."

Seek her beast? She realized after a moment that he must be talking about shifting, but she had no idea how that was supposed to help her heal.

The comment about needing to talk sounded ominous, instantly dashing the perk of pleasure his mention of a bath had given her. She nodded, staring at the toes of her boots as he strode away, while she listened to the rush of water into the pool. Finally, she tugged the boots off and tossed them aside, then rose and trudged to the bath. She discovered immediately that her muscles had stiffened while she sat. Walking was painful. She had bruises where she hadn't even realized she could have bruises.

For the first time, she was actually glad to have Damien assist her in undressing. Every movement caused a new wave of pain and it was a relief not to make the effort.

She saw, with a great deal of relief, that he had filled the pool. She was glad for that, too. No doubt the pelting water would've been good on her sore muscles, but she didn't particularly relish the thought of being pounded by anything harder than a powder puff at the moment. Gratefully, she sank into the hot water and closed her eyes.

She would've liked to simply soak until the water cooled, but she knew that at least part of that inclination was a disinclination to face Damien with what she'd done. After a few moments, therefore, she sat up and bathed. Damien was awaiting her with a towel when she stood up at last and she wondered, briefly, if he'd been there the entire time. The carpets, in the living area and scattered over the slippery tiles in the bath, muted the sound of footsteps, so it was possible. She dismissed it as unlikely, however.

He had other things on his mind at the moment. Of course, she was well aware that that probably would not last, even if he wasn't--yet. Her menses had ceased earlier in the day, and that could only mean she'd begun a new cycle. Soon, he would be aware of that, too, she felt certain.

She shuddered to think what he would make of it.

When she was dressed, he escorted her into the living area once more and indicated the couch. She sat, feeling weak still from her ordeal, from the hot bath, and, truth be told, from the look on his face.

"The assassins did not penetrate the fortress."

Khalia licked her lips nervously. "That depends upon which part you're talking about," she responded evasively.

"You were in the service area beneath the fortress when you were captured."

Khalia studied him a long moment. "Technically, I wasn't."

He gave her a look. "Why were you there instead of in your suite where you should have been?"

A spark of resentment flared, but Khalia found she couldn't maintain it in the face of his anger. "I couldn't sleep and … uh… I was bored. I decided to explore a bit."

"In that garment you arrived in?"

Khalia sent him a resentful glance. "Why don't you tell me what I was doing?"

"Trying to get yourself killed. The Regent would have my head if anything had happened to you. He might well demand it anyway, since I failed in my duty to protect you."

Khalia gaped at him. "You're not serious."

His eyes narrowed. "I am fond of my head. It does not amuse me to consider losing it." He scrubbed a hand over his face, paced for several moments and finally knelt before her. "I realize that you do not understand this world, sheashona, but you must understand that you can not be allowed to return to that other world. *I* can not allow it. You are my responsibility."

Khalia said nothing. It was almost strange to think she'd known Damien for so short a time, and stranger still that in that short a space of time he had come to mean a great deal to her. Regardless of her feelings for him, however, she refused to relinquish the hope that she could return to the world that was familiar to her. This was a frightening world, filled with even more frightening creatures and so alien to her she found that much of the time disbelief was her strongest emotion. That was no way to live. A person needed comfort at the very least, familiarity, the security of knowing what to expect at least part of the time.

After a moment, he rose stiffly and began to pace once more. "How did you open the security gate?"

Khalia looked up at him in surprise. "Gate?"

His lips tightened. "The gate that secures the lower regions of the fortress from intruders."

Khalia frowned, thinking back. "I'm not sure I did," she said finally.

He paused. "You must have. You were outside when we found you."

"Yes ... but ... one of them ... one of those creatures was behind me. He was already inside. He chased me down the corridor. I couldn't get the door, the gate, to open, not at first anyway. When it didn't open, I yelled everything I could think of to get it to open, but I'm not sure it was anything I did or said at all. When it opened, I fell through and the other creature, the one that was holding me when you arrived, grabbed me."

Damien frowned. "On your honor, this is the truth?" he asked slowly.

Khalia looked at him in surprise. "Why would I lie about that?"

"Because you think to use it again?" he suggested dryly.

Khalia gave him a look, then pursed her lips and crossed her arms, refusing to be drawn into a discussion on the fine points of acceptable lies and non-acceptable lies.

After a moment, Damien began to pace once more. "If you did not open the gate, then they were given the code by someone high in your council. Only those with the highest of positions would have the code. We have a traitor among us."

Khalia simply stared at him in disbelief. "Wait a minute!" she demanded, outraged. "You're saying those ... those things were *sent* here to kill me?"

"The Chymeria are assassins by trade," he said grimly. "They owe loyalty to no one, but neither do they kill unless it is for profit."

Khalia gaped at him. "But ... they were talking about disposing of my body across the border. You mean to say they're not enemies of the ... of Atar?"

"This fortress lies upon the border of Baklen. They are dragon folk, enemies of Atar, but they are desert people. Beyond an occasional raid, they have little interest in us ... none in politics.

"The desert is growing, however, and they either refuse to honor the original boundary, or they truly can not tell the difference, or they simply do not care and consider all desert theirs.

"Regardless, they would not have sent assassins. They might well have decided to capture you for ransom, but they would have seen no benefit in slaying you. Someone else was behind this, someone who expected the incident to erupt into a border war and cover their tracks."

Now she was an incident?

"Perhaps this explains why I have had no word from the Regent or his advisors since I sent word that we were here. I'd expected a regiment, at least, to arrive to escort you, and your household attendants. I do not think it is safe to take you to Caracaren, Princess, until we have uncovered the traitor--or traitors."

"You don't think, maybe, it would be better all the way around just to take me back to the portal and send me back? I mean, if it's going to start a war--my being here--wouldn't it be better for everybody?" Khalia said a little hopefully.

His lips thinned. "You are hereditary ruler, Princess. I do not feel that it is better, for anyone, to leave the realm in the hands of your uncle. He is not an evil man, but he is weak, swayed easily by any who would try to influence him, always yielding to his advisors, and the end result is the same. Your people need you. You can not abandon them."

It seemed useless to try to point out that she probably wouldn't be able to do any better. She knew absolutely nothing about this world, these people, or their needs. She knew nothing about governing. Beyond that, she didn't *feel* like royalty, whatever he seemed to think about it.

"We're going to stay here then?" she said, trying to keep the hopeful note out of her voice. Not that she relished the thought of another encounter such as she'd had tonight, but she didn't like the idea of traveling too far from the portal. Whatever Damien thought, she fully intended to hie herself back to Chicago at the first opportunity. Thugs aside, it seemed a safer place to be than Atar.

He studied her for several moments and finally shook his head. "If the fortress were fully manned, we could not find a better place. As it is, we can not hope to hold it against a concerted attack."

Khalia felt her heart skip several beats. "You think there'll be one?"

He shrugged. "I will not hazard a guess when your life is at stake. We must retire to a more defensible position, or a secret location until we have a better idea of what we're up against."

Chapter Nine

Khalia woke to the sound of movement close by. Despite the fact that she'd grown accustomed to finding Damien in the suite when she awoke, or finding that he'd been and left a breakfast tray, the night before had left its mark and Khalia's first reaction was fear. She bolted upright in the bed, looking around owl eyed.

Damien, whom she discovered was busily stuffing garments into a satchel he held in one hand, glanced around at her and, after staring at him blearily for several moments, Khalia collapsed back on the bed. "It can't be morning already," she muttered tiredly.

"I allowed you to sleep as long as possible. We need to be well away from here before they realize their assassins failed."

It wasn't just her imagination then, she thought. She really hadn't slept long. Groaning, she dragged herself to the edge of the bed and dropped her head in her hands. "We're leaving then?"

Damien turned to study her. His face was grim. "The guards at the eastern gate were found dead. Captain Swiftwing and his men followed the assassin's trail. They'd gone to a great deal of trouble trying to hide it, but not enough. Swiftwing ascertained that they came from Caracaren."

Shouldering the bag, he helped her to her feet and urged her toward the door. "I sent Swiftwing and his men to Caracaren to report the attempt on your life to the council. I don't know who is loyal and who is not and, until I do, I trust no one."

Khalia dug her heels in. "You expect me to leave like this?" she demanded, gesturing toward her nightgown.

He nodded, grabbing the boots she'd worn earlier and a second satchel as they passed through the living area. "You can change when we stop to rest."

To her surprise, instead of heading toward the ramparts, Damien led her toward the stairs. "We're going through the service level?" she asked in surprise, repressing a shiver.

He shook his head. "There is a secret escape passage that will take us north east of here, into the forest."

Khalia was having some difficulty shaking off the drugging effects of too little sleep, but she frowned. "Won't whoever sent the assassins know about it, too?"

"Most likely. They won't have had time to learn that the assassins failed yet, however, so it should be safe enough to use it."

"Oh … but then, what's the point?"

Damien sent her a glance of grim amusement. "It will take us in the direction I wish to go, sheashona. It was designed specifically for escape and therefore designed to hide our passage from any who would track us. They will know once they have checked the service area, of course, but it may buy us a little time."

The secret passage was in the main salon, the door a life sized rendering of a man garbed in robes and wearing a coronet. Behind the portrait was what appeared to be a clear glass globe. When Damien opened a section of the globe and gestured for her to step inside, she glanced at him a little doubtfully. After that fractional hesitation, however, she stepped into it, staring down the long shaft before her uneasily. Damien stepped in behind her, closing the door and sealing them inside. As she watched, he pressed a spot on the globe and a panel lined with buttons and switches appeared. As he flicked first one and then another, lights appeared in the shaft before them. A soft whir caught her attention and Khalia looked back in time to see a seat of sorts emerge behind Damien. Settling, Damien pulled her down until she was seated between his thighs, then pulled some sort of harness over the two of them and fastened it.

Khalia was beginning to get a very bad feeling even before she felt a vibration begin beneath them.

"What is this ... thing?"

"Escape pod," Damien said succinctly as he punched another button.

Free fall didn't begin to describe what happened next. The thing shot forward with such velocity Khalia felt as if she'd been plastered against Damien, as if she was melting into him. If she could've drawn enough air into her lungs to manage it, she would have screamed. As it was, she was thankful when she blacked out.

When consciousness returned, Khalia discovered that they had stopped. With an effort, she opened her eyes. Weak sunlight filtered through the leaves over her head. She stared up at the canopy for several moments, trying to figure out where she was and how she'd gotten there.

"You're awake."

Khalia closed her eyes at the sound of his voice, feeling anger spring instantly to life. Pushing herself upright, she glared at him. "I wasn't asleep," she ground out.

His brows rose, but he made no comment. "We need to go ... if you are feeling well enough now."

"I *feel* like killing you!" Khalia ground out. "What in God's name was that thing? And why in the hell did you decide it would be the best route of escape?"

Something gleamed in his eyes and Khalia realized that he'd actually enjoyed that thing. It made her want to kill him even more.

"In no more than twenty minutes, we traveled further than we could have walked in a day ... further than we might have flown in two hours ... without detection. We are now little more than two days' walk from our destination."

"What was that thing?" Khalia demanded. "And what demented mind thought it up?"

"The escape pod--your grandfather designed it and had it built, but it had never been used."

Khalia gaped at him. "Never been... Escape pod! You said escape *route*. You never said anything about a pod and I can't *believe* you put me in that thing when it had never even been tested!"

Damien got to his feet. "I said it had not been used. It was exhaustively tested."

Khalia climbed shakily to her feet, as well. "My grandfather ... you put me in something my *grandfather* built before I was even born?"

He nodded. "You were not harmed," he pointed out.

"I passed out from pure terror. Do you know how many times in my life I've passed out from pure terror?"

He lifted a brow questioningly.

Khalia ground her teeth. Stalking toward him until they were toe to toe, she plunked her hands on her hips and glared up at him. "Once!"

One corner of his lips twitched. "You are enchanting when you are angry, sheashona."

Khalia let out a growl and kicked him on the shin. Unfortunately, she'd forgotten she was bare foot. He was wearing boots. Yelping, she grabbed her throbbing toe, hopping on one foot. Damien caught her shoulders to steady her. Dropping her injured foot, she gave him an angry shove. He didn't move, but the force of her blow set her off balance. He caught her, jerking her tightly against his chest. When Khalia tilted her head up to glare at him, she saw that the amusement had vanished from his expression. In its place was a purposefulness that set her heart to hammering in her chest and made her mouth go dry. As she watched, she saw the muscles of his throat convulse on a hard swallowed. Lifting a hand, he stroked her cheek lightly. "Will it make you feel better if I say I was as frightened as you were?"

Khalia licked her dry lips. "You weren't," she said a little doubtfully.

He studied the movement of her tongue, his eyes darkening. Finally, he dropped his hand to her arm and nodded. "The force from the speed was more than I'd expected. When you went limp, I thought I'd killed you. I'm more relieved than I can say that you woke ready to take me to task for frightening you."

Khalia looked away, feeling disappointment fill her. She'd hoped he meant to kiss her. She drew in a shuddering breath. "I shouldn't have lost my temper. I … misunderstood. I thought you were familiar with the … uh … escape thingy."

As if he'd only just become aware that he still held her tightly against him, his arms relaxed, his hands settling along her waist as if he would set her away from him. Khalia looked up at him and smiled faintly. Lifting a hand, she placed it on his chest. "I'm more glad than I can say that I have you…." She stumbled to a halt at the look that came into his eyes. "That it was you who found me," she finished a little breathlessly.

His hands clenched on her waist almost painfully, as if he was of two minds, one to push her away, and the other to pull her tightly against him once more. The latter won out. Slipping his arms around her, he molded her tightly against him, dipping his head to nuzzle the side of her neck, and then the shell of her ear. Finally, he caught a fistful of her hair and tipped her head back, covering her mouth with the urgency of long denied hunger.

Khalia's heart seemed to stop in her chest as he filled her world with himself. The heat of his mouth sent pleasure coursing through her. She sucked in a shaky breath as her heart commenced to hammering erratically, beating out a desperate tattoo of need that burgeoned, filling the darkest, most secret recesses of her being. Her fingers curled against his chest as his tongue skated along her lips, seeking, she realized instinctively, to caress her more intimately.

Opening her mouth to him, she slipped her arms upward, locking her hands behind his head and surging upward on her toes to give him greater access, flattening her breasts against his hard chest. A shudder of delight went through her as he thrust his tongue possessively inside her mouth, raking it along her own. She moved restlessly against him.

The thin gown she wore had never seemed substantial enough and now felt like far too much of a barrier between them. Through it, the heat and strength of his body, the texture of his skin teased her. Her nipples tightened, hardening, extending to become acute sensors, and shards of pleasure pulsed from the brushing contact, joining the rush of delight created by the feel and taste of his tongue as he explored her mouth thoroughly to become a massive influx of wondrous, debilitating sensation. Enthralled, she pressed closer until her lower body brushed his, and she felt the heated length of his manhood pressing into the softness of her belly.

Dimly, she realized she should have been appalled by the blatant evidence of his arousal. She should have felt some alarm at the size of it. Instead, she felt her body clench with need and her heart flutter in anticipation. A shudder went through her as he skated one hand down her spine, molding her body against his own until, finally, he cupped one buttock, lifting and pulling her against him in a rhythmic, erotic massage that ground her pubic bone against his hard length. With each thrust, a sense of desperation began to build in her, an expanding and contracting of her senses that she knew, instinctively, was leading her somewhere she wanted to go.

Abruptly, he tore his mouth from hers, burying it against her neck, sucking the sensitive flesh in a way that sent a flurry of sensation rippling over the skin of her neck and shoulder. His hand tightened on her buttock, pressing her hard against him and holding her for several heartbeats.

She sensed his withdrawal even though he held still held her closely, felt the tension in his body as he held himself rigidly still for many moments, breathing raggedly. The snap of a twig nearby sent a jolt through both of them and Damien lifted his head, looking around sharply.

Abruptly, he set her away from him. "This is insanity," he growled almost angrily. Moving away from her, he snatched the packs off the ground and shouldered them.

Khalia shivered as he moved away from her, watching his angry, jerky movements in a fog of confusion. He refused to meet her eye. Instead, he caught her upper arm and led her away from the small clearing. Khalia glanced behind them as he tugged her away. There was no sign of the tube, no sign of the pod. Around them, there was only the thick vegetation of a primal forest. Within moments, she couldn't even see the small clearing.

He released her after a moment, holding the brush aside with his arms as they passed through it. Perhaps ten minutes had passed when she heard the gurgle of rushing water that announced the presence of a stream ahead of them. Still wrapped in the cocoon of shock created by his abrupt dismissal, Khalia continued to stumble along behind him, unable to think, or to feel beyond a growing sense of pain and anger at his rejection. She didn't realize that they'd reached the stream until Damien stepped into it.

Slipping on the damp vegetation at the edge, Khalia landed in the stream up to her neck. The shock of the chilled water stole the breath from her lungs. She was still gasping for air when Damien pulled her to her feet. His hands tightened on her when she'd gained her feet instead of releasing her. Peering at him through the damp strings of her hair, she saw that his gaze was fixed on the wet, clinging fabric that now covered far less even than it had when dry.

After a moment, he swallowed convulsively and released her. "We need to follow the stream to throw them off our scent."

Khalia gaped at him while outrage slowly supplanted her shock. After bringing her to the point where she was ready to throw caution and morals to the wind and roll around in the grass with him, rutting like an animal, *this* was all he could think of to say to her?

"Are you up to it?" he persisted when she said nothing.

Khalia's eyes narrowed, her lips thinning as rage began simmering inside of her.

Damien flushed, but she wasn't certain whether it was from embarrassment or if his own anger had flared when she remained mute, and she didn't particularly care.

He looked away. "The stream branches in every direction. Even if they follow us to this point, they won't be able to determine which direction we've taken. If we have enough of a lead on them, the trail will grow cold."

Without a word, Khalia untied the ties at the side of the gown and peeled it off, carefully bundling the sodden mass of fabric into a ball. Damien stared at her as if she'd lost her mind. She heaved the soaked gown at his head, feeling a measure of satisfaction as the soggy bundle slapped him in the face. "I won't be needing this," she said tightly, side stepping him and slogging down the stream in the lead.

She felt his heated gaze on her back, but many moments passed before she heard the splash that told her he was following. By the time it filtered through her enraged mind that he was closing the distance between them at a speed that indicated she'd managed to arouse his ire, it was too late to react. She yelped as he seized her around the waist and snatched her off her feet. Before she'd managed to place more than a glancing blow in her defense, he deposited her, none too gently, on a mossy bank. The boots he'd been carrying hit the bank beside her and right behind it a pack. She glared at him, her chest heaving with fury.

His gaze slid over her and away again. "Get dressed."

Khalia wasn't certain what demon of mischief prompted her, but it was not simply a matter of 'too mad to care'. She not only made no attempt to guard her modesty, she very deliberately provoked him by simply remaining just as she was, her legs splayed before her, glaring back at him until he turned to look at her once more. When she had his full attention, she grasped one of the boots and slowly pulled it on as his gaze moved over her and finally settled on the damp thatch of red hair between her thighs. She paused when she had it on, pretending to adjust it for several moments before she picked up the second boot and pulled it on just as slowly.

By the time she reached for the pack, Damien looked in imminent danger of a heart attack. He was breathing raggedly, his chest heaving with each struggling breath. His eyes were black with desire, glazed.

With deliberation, she searched the pack, discarding first one garment and then another until, with a growl of frustration, Damien stalked away. A satisfied smile curled her lips. Picking up one of the kerchief-like tops, she tied it behind her head and then secured the remaining tie behind her back. It seemed pointless to put on one of the skirts if they were to be slogging through water. A brief search turned up a garment similar to the one Damien wore, except that it was no more than a narrow strip in the back, which fit between her buttocks. She got up and stepped into it, pulling it up. When Damien paused at last to look back, she turned her back to him, bent over at the waist and began to put the discarded garments back into it with a pretense of unconcern.

He was glaring at her when she straightened and turned with the pack in her hand. Without a word, he sloshed back across the stream, snatched the pack from her hand and stalked away again.

Khalia's sense of satisfaction waned as the day wore on and they followed the stream to a fork and turned, following the branch for hours it seemed, for miles. She'd had almost no sleep--she doubted Damien had had any at all--and she thought it was probably far more work to walk in the shallow stream even than it would have been to fight their way through the heavy brush of the forest.

Instead of stopping for lunch, Damien pulled a wrapped bundle from the pack and peeled the metallic wrapping back. Revealing what looked to be a small loaf of bread, he tore it in half and handed her a piece. Khalia looked it over and discovered that some kind of meat and cheese had been stuffed inside the bread. The meat tasted like beef or perhaps lamb, although she thought it was probably doubtful that either creature existed on this world. They ate in silence, just as they'd walked in silence. When Khalia had finished, she stopped and scooped up handfuls of water to quench her thirst. Damien stopped to drink, as well, his gaze flickering over her, both desire and, strangely, puzzlement clouding his features.

Khalia found she was too tired to try to figure out what the look might mean or even to care. Her body warmed beneath his gaze, despite her weariness, however, and irritation surfaced. Swiping the water from her mouth, she moved ahead of him again, ignoring the temptation to tease him.

She discovered when she finally glanced back to see why he wasn't following her, that wasn't necessary to put any effort into it. The outfit she'd chosen was obviously provocative enough by itself, for his gaze was caught by the hypnotic sway of her bare buttocks. When she stopped, he blinked, stared down at the drops of water drying on his fingers for several moments and finally surged forward and past her, setting an even more grueling pace than before.

Several times throughout the afternoon Khalia was tempted to call after him and demand that he slow down. She found she was reluctant to do so, however. Angry as she was, she merely bit her tongue and did her best to keep up, ignoring the fact that he was getting further and further ahead of her. By the time dusk began closing in around her, Khalia had become so tired she'd long since lost all awareness of anything except picking one foot up and putting it down again. It wasn't until the first croak of some water creature snapped her out of her misery that she realized she couldn't even hear Damien in front of her any more.

Chapter Ten

Khalia stopped abruptly, looking around in surprise, wondering if she'd taken a turn down some narrow stream when Damien went straight … or gone straight when he'd turned off. She was on the point of calling out to him when it occurred to her that predators, or assassins, might be closer to her than Damien was. Even if they weren't, her cry could give away their position if anyone other than Damien was close enough to hear.

Fear crept insidiously through her veins as she stood indecisively, jumping at each little sound, straining to hear some sound that would indicate Damien's direction. Lifting her head, she strained to listen, struggled to hear something that would give her hope. Instead, as she stood frozen in the middle of the stream, realizing she was no longer even certain of which direction she'd come from, or which she'd been traveling in, she heard the distant splash of something really large hitting the water.

Her heart leapt out of her chest and lodged itself in her throat as she looked wildly around, envisioning something like a giant snake, or an alligator swimming swiftly toward her.

Stifling the urge to scream, she whirled and fled away from the sound, the need to stay silent and remain in the stream fixed so firmly in her mind that she fought the instinct to do either, or both, silently racing along the stream bed as fast as she could. Her heart felt as if it would burst, from both exhaustion and fear. An internal darkness, as dangerous as the oncoming night, threatened the edges of her vision. A fiery pain developed in her side that became harder and harder to ignore.

Suddenly, someone, or something, seized her from behind. Gasping, she whirled and fought with what little remained of her flagging strength.

"Cease! Sheashona!" He gave her a slight shake when she continued to fight his hold mindlessly.

Finally, his voice filtered through the maze of terror that gripped her mind and Khalia went limp against him, too weak and shaken even to cling to him for support. He pulled her tightly against him, holding her until the tremors that shook her began to subside.

"Heard something," she managed to gasp, uncertain now whether or not it had been Damien that she'd heard, but fearful that it hadn't been and the threat was still there.

Damien stiffened, suddenly alert as he glanced around them. Scooping her into his arms, he moved swiftly to the bank and emerged from the stream.

A spark of anger flared, that he'd left her behind, but she was too weak and exhausted even to fan it and it died almost as quickly as it had flickered to life. Instead of subsiding, the tremors grew worse until her teeth were chattering. Even the warmth of Damien's body failed to chase the chill away.

Finally, he stopped. Khalia lifted her head with an effort and looked around. They were in a tiny clearing, she saw. Their packs lay beside a shelter of some sort, fashioned of branches and leaves.

"I didn't think it wise to build a fire, but perhaps I should build a small one--at least until you're warm."

Khalia shook her head, pulling away from him and struggling to be put down. She braced her knees as he slowly lowered her to the ground. "I'm just a little c-chilled," she managed to say with barely a stammer. "I was…." She broke off, swallowing against the sudden urge to cry like a baby in the aftermath. "I was just …," she tried again.

She felt her face crumple when he hooked a finger beneath her chin and forced her to look up at him. "I was scared!" she wailed, giving up the effort to try to remain stoic. "I couldn't see you anymore, and then I got turned around and I heard something and I didn't know which way to run."

He pulled her against his chest, wrapping his arms tightly around her until she'd regained control of her wayward emotions and the trembling had begun to subside.

Khalia was grateful for it, and for the warmth that slowly seeped inside of her, replacing the chill. Finally, sniffing, she pushed against him. Almost reluctantly, he relaxed his grip on her and finally allowed his arms to drop as she stepped away from him. "I'm sorry," she mumbled. "Ordinarily, I'm not like this at all. I'm usually so … in control." But then, she wasn't usually faced with the sort of things she'd had to face since she'd arrived here … not that

that was an excuse. She should have been able to handle the little bumps in the road she'd encountered. It wasn't as if her life had been smoothing sailing before all of this had happened.

But then, Damien had introduced her to a whole range of emotions she'd never felt before.

Still more than a little weak kneed, she half sat, half collapsed on the ground in front of the shelter. After staring at her for several moments, Damien grabbed up the pack that contained their food and sat down across from her. "You're certain you don't want a fire?" he asked slowly.

She shook her head, then nodded a little jerkily. "No. I'm fine. Really."

Opening the pack at last, he pulled out another bundle like the one he'd taken from it earlier. Khalia held out her hand to stop him when he would've torn it in half. "You eat it. I'm … actually, I'm not really hungry."

He frowned. "You need the food for strength."

She didn't feel like arguing with him. "A small piece then."

He tore off half and handed it to her. She studied it a long moment and finally divided it in half again and handed one portion back to him. He looked at it, but didn't take it. She shrugged and acted as if she was going to toss it aside. Grabbing her wrist, he took the offering and, after giving her a reproachful glance, ate it.

"I'm far more thirsty than hungry," she said around a small bite of food. "Which I suppose is silly considering we've waded water all day."

Without a word, he produced a metal container and handed it to her. Twisting the lid off, she sniffed it, discovered it was water and drank several draughts before she set the container down between them and finished off the portion of food she'd taken. Brushing the crumbs from her hands, she picked up the container and took another couple of sips, then set it between them again.

She'd almost decided he meant the container strictly for her use when he picked it up. Something fluttered in her stomach when she saw his lips curl around the neck of the container as hers had only moments before. The memory of the way his lips had felt on hers flooded her with remembered warmth. She looked away, studying the crude shelter. "I guess this means we sleep here?"

He cleared his throat. When she glanced at him, she saw that he was twisting the lid back on the container, a frown pulling his brows together. "You need to rest."

She wasn't going to argue with him. She'd thought she was fit enough to handle most anything. She'd been accustomed to walking the ten blocks from her apartment to the museum regularly, taking a cab only when she stayed late or when the weather was inclement. Today had been a test of endurance, however, and she ached in places she hadn't even known she *had* muscles. "You need to rest, too."

"I'll stand guard."

She was suddenly angry. "And you'll be useless to either of us if you mean to be so pig headed and refuse to rest."

He sent her a startled glance and flushed. "I am a soldier. I am accustomed to forced marches."

"In a pig's eye! You fly! You don't slog through swamps all day like today."

A hint of amusement gleamed momentarily in his eyes before he resolutely extinguished it. "It's not safe to fly. We'd be too easy to spot."

"I'm not arguing the logic of walking," Khalia said testily. "I'm not a fool, despite what you obviously think … never mind. Suit yourself … but you might want to consider that *I* can't carry you … you big ox!"

Turning her back on him, she crawled into the shelter and lay down with her back to the opening. To her surprise, it was actually quite comfortable. Damien had piled soft vegetation all over the ground beneath the shelter and undoubtedly taken the time to remove any hard objects. She sincerely hoped the leaves weren't crawling with biting insects. It occurred to her after a moment that she hadn't been bitten at all, despite the fact that they'd been traipsing through woods all day. Either this world had no biting insects--utopian dream!--or they were few and far between, and/or didn't have a taste for her hide.

She'd begun to drowse when Damien climbed into the shelter behind her. She shifted to give him more room as he struggled to settle in the small space, but resisted the urge to smile, uncertain of whether or not he might be able to see it.

Naturally, it was black as pitch inside the tiny shelter, but she'd misjudged his dragon senses before. She knew now that, even when he appeared to be no more than human, as she was, he possessed senses that went beyond those of humans.

When he finally settled, leaving as much distance between them as the shelter allowed, she turned over, lifted the arm he wasn't laying on and placed it over her waist, then snuggled close to him.

"Sheashona," he whispered hoarsely.

"I'm cold," she responded plaintively.

He released a long suffering sigh. "I will build a fire."

"No. This is good."

She heard him grind his teeth as she slipped an arm around his waist and worked one thigh between his legs. Yawning as his warmth slowly enveloped her, she relaxed and allowed sleep to overtake her.

Light was filtering through the opening when Khalia woke as Damien carefully disentangled himself and climbed out of the shelter. Khalia sighed, reluctant to move, but the morning air was cool and her heat had escaped her clutches. She stretched and was immediately sorry as every muscle in her body protested with agony. Groaning, she crawled out and looked around. Damien was no where to be seen. Shrugging, she went a little way into the brush to relieve herself and then listened until she determined the direction of the stream.

They were not far from it, but when she'd washed her face and hands and scrubbed her teeth the best she could with her finger she discovered that she wasn't sure of which direction to take to get back to the clearing. "This is embarrassing," she muttered, plunking her hands on her hips and looking around. She hadn't realized she had such a poor sense of direction. Of course, she'd never been in a situation like this. She'd spent her whole life in a city. She knew the city and even if by some wild chance she'd managed to get herself lost, she knew all she had to do was hail a cab. There were no cabs here, no street signs, no people to ask her way. She couldn't even see the sun through the trees.

Finally, she sat down again, pulled her boots off and dabbled her feet in the water.

Damien, she knew, would come to look for her.

He looked ready to breathe fire when he found her some fifteen minutes later. She sent him a look of surprise. Without a word, he grasped her arms and hauled her to her feet. "Do you have a death wish?" he growled.

Khalia frowned, discovering it was still far too early for her to ignore this sort of provocation. "No," she said tightly.

"Then don't wander off!" he growled, shaking his finger under her nose as if she was naughty child.

Khalia bit him. She hadn't actually intended to do more than nip at him. She wasn't even certain of where the impulse had come from. She just did it before she thought better of it, as if someone, or something, was controlling her.

Damien yelped, snatching his finger back and examining it.

Khalia bit her lip, trying to subdue the urge to laugh.

He glared at her in outrage.

She managed to look repentant. "I'm sorry. I don't know what made me do that. Here. Let me see."

They fought a short tug of war over the abused appendage. Finally, Damien, apparently deciding his dignity had suffered enough, thrust the finger out for her to examine it.

To her relief, she saw she hadn't broken the skin. She supposed it was surprise more than anything else that had caused him to jerk his finger away, but, driven by her new resident demon, she leaned closer and kissed it. "Better," she asked, looking up at him innocently.

He swallowed, his eyes darkening.

It was all the inspiration her demon needed. Very deliberately, she lifted his finger and slipped it between her lips, sucking on it.

The air rushed from his chest as if she'd rammed her fist into his solar plexus. Releasing his finger the moment he tugged at it, she turned and sat down, pulling her boots on. "I don't suppose we could eat before we start?"

Either he didn't hear her or he chose to ignore her, leaping into the stream hard enough to splatter her thoroughly with water. She gasped as the cold water hit her, but resolutely refused to look up at him and allow him to see he'd succeeded in annoying her.

He stalked away without a word, muttering under his breath.

"What?" Khalia called.

He stopped and turned slowly, frowning.

"I thought you said something."

His lips tightened. "The god's willing we should reach our destination by the morrow," he growled and turned away once more.

Khalia hurried after him, keeping pace with an effort. "Where are we going?"

He threw her an irritated glance. "My brother's holdings."

"Do you have any sisters?"

"No. Thank the gods, I do not."

"Nasty," Khalia muttered.

He slid a glance in her direction but refused to be baited.

"Just the one brother?" Khalia persisted.

"Two brothers, Nigel and Basil."

"No one else?"

"No."

Khalia lapsed into silence, wondering if he really meant no one, or if there was a female, or females, somewhere that he wasn't counting. Not that it mattered. He'd made it clear enough that he had no desire to give in to his attraction to her--and, when all was said and done, she was afraid it wasn't a very powerful attraction to start with if he could ignore it so easily. The Lord only knew she'd done everything she could think of to break through his determined resistance.

She supposed that was the problem, the well from whence her demons sprang. It wounded her ego that he was the first man she'd met in her life that had tempted her beyond reason, and she hadn't been able to tempt him beyond reason.

It wasn't entirely her ego, however, and she knew it. Her feelings ran deeper than desires of the flesh. It hurt that he seemed to have no interest in her beyond seeing to it that she was installed as his damned queen.

It occurred to her, too, that she felt strangely unlike herself. She wasn't certain why, but it was almost as if she had a beast within her as he did and it had begun to control her instead of the other way around.

Was it even remotely possible that what he'd said was true? Or was it something like wishful thinking on her part, that she'd stumbled upon her roots in a place she had never expected to find them?

Sighing, she gave up the effort to keep pace with him and set her own pace, wondering how far they were now from the portal. She wouldn't have wanted to stay in this place even if it hadn't been for the fact that she'd found herself in the middle of some sort of political intrigue. She certainly had no desire to get herself killed over something she'd never wanted to begin with.

Maybe his brother would be more reasonable? It was worth a try anyway. As accustomed as she was to being self-sufficient, she wasn't a fool. She knew her limitations and it was obvious she wasn't going to make it back to the portal without help. She might have had some chance of it if she'd managed to get out of the fortress Damien had taken her to. She knew it couldn't have been far. Now, the further they went, the more remote her chances became.

The only bright spot that she could see was that she had the power to torment Damien almost as much as he annoyed her.

When she glanced up, she saw that he was rapidly disappearing from sight. Shrugging, she ignored him, glancing at the forest on either side of the creek as flashes of color caught her eye. She hadn't been in any condition to pay much attention to her surroundings the day before. In truth, she was a city girl through and through and not particularly drawn to nature anyway, but she discovered she was curious about this world.

Trees and shrubs grew thickly, right down to the water line. She didn't have a clue whether or not they looked anything like plants that might be found in similar areas of her own world, but she was fairly certain the color differed. All the leaves she could see were a bright green, varying from a shade more yellow than green to an almost teal color, but there were no true greens.

The song of a bird caught her attention and she paused, studying the brush closely for a look at it. When she caught a glimpse of it at last, she felt a welling inside of her almost like … joy. It was a tiny thing, moving like quicksilver among the branches, but pausing now and then to trill out it's lovely warble. It was green, which she supposed accounted for the difficulty in spotting it, beyond its size. It had a jaunty little cockade, though, of bright red, which curled over one of its bright blue eyes.

"Is something amiss?"

Khalia looked at Damien a little guiltily. "I stopped to rest a moment," she lied. "And I saw that little bird. What is it?"

Frowning, Damien turned to follow the direction of her finger. He flushed and looked away. "I don't see anything."

Puzzled by his strange reaction, Khalia glanced toward the bird again. "There. See it? It's almost the same color as the leaves…but it's such a pretty little thing."

Damien let out a long suffering sigh. "It's a sheashona," he said shortly.

Khalia glanced at him in surprise. "But…."

"If we don't make better time, we will spend two more nights on the trail," he cut in shortly. Reaching for her hand, he clasped it firmly in his own and tugged her into motion once more. Khalia slid a couple of glances in his direction, saw that he was studiously ignoring her and allowed herself a faint smile.

Chapter Eleven

Khalia wasn't certain whether they made good time or
not. The streams they'd been following the day before had
never gotten much deeper than mid-calf. In truth, the mud
sucking at the soles of her boots had made the going harder
than the resistance of the water they were wading through.
By mid afternoon, however, the branch they followed on
their second day was nearly to her knees and growing
steadily deeper.

Damien took care that she didn't fall too far behind him.
Each time he noticed that she'd dropped back, he stopped,
waiting until she caught up to him and then grasped her
hand and tugged her along behind him. As the water
deepened, they made less and less progress, but Khalia
refrained from complaining and Damien continued until
darkness began to close in. Finally, they waded out. Khalia
dropped to the bank as soon as they reached it, tugging her
boots off and pouring the water out. After a moment,
Damien settled beside her and emptied his own boots.
"We'll travel overland from here."

Khalia nodded, too tired to care at the moment. Her feet,
she saw, were pruned and white from the water. She didn't
particularly want to put the boots back on, but she knew the
skin would tear easily in its current condition. "I don't
suppose we could just sleep here?" she asked a little
hopefully, tugging the boots on once more.

"It would not be wise. Animals come to the stream to
drink at night."

"All right then," Khalia said, getting up at once and
looking around alertly.

Damien's lips twitched, but he said nothing, merely
turning and pushing through the brush. Khalia followed as
closely behind him as she could, allowing him to clear the
way for her. Finally, after about a half an hour, they came

upon a small clearing and Damien stopped, looking it over speculatively.

As *if* they had a lot of choices! Khalia thought irritably, finding a spot near the center and collapsing. *I'm going to die in this godforsaken place*, she thought morosely as she stared up at the little patch of sky she could see through the trees. If Damien didn't walk her to death, something was going to eat her, an assassin was going to get her, or a hoard of horny dragons was going to swoop down, fall on her like a pack of dogs and screw her to death.

Any time now, Damien was going to tumble to the fact that she was smack in the middle of another reproductive cycle--probably along about the time that the horny hoard arrived because he was hell bent and determined to ignore her. She supposed she should have warned him, but she hadn't felt comfortable talking about female things with a man, and it wasn't as if either one of them could actually do anything about it.

When Damien began flattening an area of brush, she sat up, watching him for several moments before she rose tiredly and went to help. He left her flattening the brush and moved to a nearby tree, pulling vines from it. When he returned, he dropped the vines to the ground and began bending the saplings that surrounded the area they'd flattened, tying them together with the vines. Once he'd formed a frame with the bent saplings, he began hacking low hanging branches from other trees around the clearing and piling them on the frame.

Khalia was impressed. Within a very short while they not only had a reasonably comfortable shelter, but there was also very little damage to the environment. "Where did you learn how to do this?"

He shrugged. "Trial and error. My brothers and I spent a good deal of time in the forest hunting when we were youngsters."

Khalia smiled faintly, picturing a young Damien running around the woods playing...what? Not cowboys and Indians--but very likely something of that nature. Damien looked at her questioningly. She shook her head. "I was just thinking--people always think that people from other cultures aren't like them at all, when the truth is they probably have more in common than there are differences."

Damien frowned. "We are of the same culture … the same race."

Khalia sighed. "The same race … maybe, but I'm still not convinced, and definitely not the same culture. If I hadn't studied similar cultures, I wouldn't have a clue of what was going on, and, as it is, text book knowledge isn't the same as knowing and experiencing something." She shook her head. "Maybe I'm too different ever to fit in here. Have you considered that?"

Damien studied her a long moment and finally turned his attention to distributing the food from the pack. "You have the intelligence to learn. All you need is the desire."

She had plenty of desire, but not the sort he was referring to, she felt certain. She rolled her eyes. "Exactly what do you think has happened here to give me any desire to want to be here?" she said irritably.

He flushed. "You will be queen," he pointed out.

"If somebody doesn't kill me first. *And*, I should point out, that's not something I ever aspired to and I don't find the prospect all that thrilling even if I *should* be made queen."

"You have no sense of … duty to your family name, to your people?"

Khalia studied him a long moment. "Do you have any idea of what an orphanage is? Or what it's like?"

He frowned thoughtfully. "The word isn't familiar."

"It's, basically, a warehouse for children. They put all the unwanted children together. They're sheltered, fed, educated and then turned out to make their own way in the world when they're old enough. The people that take care of you do it because it's their job. They get paid for it. They don't actually *care* about you. They don't want to, because if they did and you were sent away, or someone adopted you, then they'd be sad, so mostly they just figure it's better to remain emotionally distant.

"So, to answer your question, no, I don't. I'd have to care about them before I felt anything like that, and I honestly don't. I didn't *care* about the people in the world I grew up in. I sure as hell don't care anything about the people responsible for making my life what it was … if they had anything to do with it, which you say they did."

"You will feel differently once you have had time to adjust."

Khalia sighed and finally just shrugged. The truth was, there was only one thing she could think of that might make being here worth while, and it seemed to her that the chance of it was remote. Moreover, she'd begun to realize that it was almost certainly for the best. This didn't seem like a very healthy place for her and she didn't need her judgment clouded by emotions that might get her killed. The life she'd had might have been boring, but, mostly anyway, it hadn't been threatening either.

In fact, if she hadn't been so determined to hang on to the talisman that had been left to her by her mother, none of this would have happened at all … which just went to show how dangerous any sort of sentiment was.

"I'm tired," she announced abruptly and got up and went into the shelter. She didn't invite Damien to join her or try to coax him. She rather thought she preferred that he didn't. She'd been playing a dangerous game without even realizing it. She was far too fond of Damien already. She shouldn't have been pushing him to try to get to know him better. She certainly shouldn't have been trying to encourage him toward greater intimacy. That road would lead to nothing but pain for her and possibly worse for him.

Typically, he followed her, settling behind her where she lay on the bedding of fresh grasses and pulling her close. She might not know anything about relationships, but she'd figured out a long time ago that people were contrary creatures. You couldn't beg them to take something you wanted to give away, but the very moment you showed any indication that you didn't want them to have it, it became something they desired above all else.

He was warm, though, and the nights were chilly. He made her feel safe, protected--and that was all she needed to feel completely relaxed and find sleep.

She faced the following day with mixed feelings. Today, Damien had said they would arrive at the safe house. She was exhausted, and looking forward to doing absolutely nothing for a while--maybe not even getting out of bed. She was also glad that there would be others around, a buffer between herself and Damien. It would make it easier for her to distance herself from him.

She was sorry for the same reason, regretful to give up the bond they'd formed … or at least the bond she'd formed. She could hardly speak for Damien. In fact, as far as she could tell he was even more anxious to reach his brother's holdings than she was. He set a grueling pace. She kept up the best she could, more because he was breaking through the brush than because she felt any need to prove she *could* keep up, or because of any fear that he'd leave her and she would get lost.

Fat chance of him allowing *that*!

It was harder, she quickly discovered, plowing through the brush than it had been slogging through the streams. They stopped to rest briefly while they ate and then pushed on again. The sun was already dropping toward the horizon when they broke from the forest at last and stopped on a rise. Below them lay acres and acres of cultivated fields. The rise they stood on climbed sharply just north of where they stood. A jumble of rocks, looking strangely out of place, topped the hill.

As they skirted the edge of the field, Khalia studied the mound they were heading toward and realized finally that the reason the rocks looked so out of place was because they seemed to have been pushed up from below, or carted there and piled. There was no mountain above them to explain their presence. Perhaps something like an ice age?

Damien stopped when they reached the foot of the pile, studying it with his hands on his hips. After a few moments, he turned and studied the sky and the fields that surrounded them. Finally, taking her hand, he began climbing.

Puzzled, Khalia merely followed him, concentrating on keeping her balance. Finally, he stopped again and slipped his hand into a narrow crevice. Abruptly, the stone in front of them, which was roughly half the size of a car, slid open, revealing a dark hole. When they'd stepped inside, the ceiling illuminated and the door closed again.

They were in a narrow corridor that looked as if it had been hewn from the stones. They followed it for what seemed two miles at least and came at last upon another door. Beside this door was a panel with buttons on it.

It looked an awful lot like the panel in the 'pod' and Khalia was on the point of balking when the door slid open and she saw a great, darkened room. As they stepped through the portal, several wall sconces flared to life. A shiver crept up her spine. It looked like a dungeon.

And it was guarded by a creature that no one could have imagined in their worst nightmare.

Roughly the size and probably the weight of a half grown elephant, the similarity to any creature known to mankind ended there. It had six legs, each ending in a paw with three razor sharp looking claws. Sharp, quill-looking spines covered its entire body. Its head was broad and wedge shaped, its jaw wide and filled with about twice as many teeth as it could possibly have needed. A single, elongated eye curved around its bony head, appearing to give the thing at least a 160 degree viewing angle.

Khalia froze as the thing leapt to its feet and bolted toward them as if it would gulp them down in a single swallow, too frightened to move even before it occurred to her that running probably wasn't wise or even an option. It skidded to a halt in front of Damien, sniffed him suspiciously for a moment and then began to gyrate and dance around him, snuffling and licking at his legs, back and belly.

Grinning, Damien clubbed in on top of its head with his fist. "Down!"

He turned to Khalia and motioned for her to walk toward him. Khalia looked at him and then the, now cowed, nightmare. She didn't move.

Damien frowned. "He won't hurt you."

"Not if I don't get close enough …. What is that thing?"

"A garshon. He is well trained and he knows me. Come. I will introduce you to him."

"Ahh … Thanks, but I don't think so."

Damien gave her an exasperated look and moved toward her purposefully. The moment he started toward her the beast leapt up and rushed her, snarling and slavering. Damien caught it by a spiked collar Khalia hadn't noticed when she was staring at its huge, yellow, pointed teeth. "No, Zakiah!" He turned to look at her again. "He must learn your scent so that he will know you as a friend."

Khalia thought she'd rather not, but it was obvious the thing served as a guard dog for the lower regions of what she supposed must be his brother's holdings. After a moment, she held her hand out. The thing sniffed her suspiciously, licked her hand and then looked up at Damien with a 'please master, may I eat it?' look.

Damien released his grip on the animal's collar and pulled Khalia close to his side. "Friend, Zakiah!"

Zakiah looked from Damien to Khalia and back again several times and finally, a look of disappointment clouding its features, it slunk off into the darkness once more.

"You think it took? The recognition thing?"

Damien shrugged. "You'll know the first time you come down here alone."

Khalia sent him a startled glance, saw that his eyes were dancing with amusement and elbowed him in the ribs. "Very humorous!"

He chuckled. "He will not forget, or allow anyone who is not a friend near you so long as he has breath to defend you. Garshon are generally not tamable. My brother and I found him when he was very young, however, and raised him. He will allow no one in here except us … and now you."

Khalia glanced around at the thing crouching in the dark a little doubtfully. "You think ... just because you introduced me to that thing that its not going to try to eat me the next time?"

"My scent is all over you. He believes you are mine."

Startled, Khalia glanced at Damien, but forbore comment. It occurred to her to wonder, though, if the animal could be so easily fooled.

Taking her hand, Damien led her toward a narrow stone stair that wound upward. At the top, the door was opened before they reached it. The man that stood in the doorway was very similar in build to Damien and around the same height. His hair was more brown than black, however, and he looked to be a few years older than Damien.

"Nigel!"

A faint smile curved Nigel's lips. He grasped Damien's extended arm as he surged forward, giving Damien a jerk that brought them together like a clap of thunder. They embraced, pounding each other on the back. Khalia winced at the meaty thuds but apparently they both enjoyed it hugely. Both men were grinning when they finally drew apart once more.

A wave of envy washed over Khalia when Damien turned to look at her, holding his hand out, envy for the obvious affection between the two brothers, something she'd never had the chance to experience, and, more specifically, envy of Damien's love. Smiling with an effort, she extended her hand and placed it in Damien's outstretched one. "Princess Khalia--may I present my brother, Nigel."

"Your highness." Nigel knelt, saluting her.

Khalia felt color climbing her cheeks. "Thank you for allowing me to come," she said uncomfortably, and then glanced at Damien self-consciously, wondering if Nigel *had* allowed it, or if Damien had merely anticipated an invitation that hadn't been extended.

"I'd expected the two of you earlier," Nigel replied, easing Khalia's discomfort immediately. Turning, he summoned a woman. Khalia studied the woman uncertainly, wondering if she was a servant, or Nigel's wife. "Charrisa. Show the princess to her room and make sure she has everything she needs."

Khalia was grateful. She could well imagine she looked unkempt, to say the very least, after their trek through the wilderness. As much as the promised treat pleased her, though, she discovered that she was more than a little reluctant to leave Damien's side. She quelled it irritably, following the servant without even glancing in Damien's direction, though it took a strenuous effort.

The apartment Charrisa led her to was elegant although not nearly as opulent as the royal suite she'd occupied at the fortress. In truth, Khalia was relieved. She'd felt like a fraud living in the princess' quarters. This apartment, although far richer than anything she'd occupied in her life before coming to Atar, seemed more comfortable, more like the sort of place one could actually live in rather being displayed.

The bath was equally elegant, and yet not overwhelming. Charrisa ran her bath and helped her to undress. Khalia didn't particularly want help, but she'd come to realize that her resistance to accepting the customs here only made everyone around her uncomfortable and added to her own discomfort, making her feel more out of place.

When she'd bathed, she found that Charrisa had laid out a sleeping gown for her. "Master Nigel thought you might want to rest before dinner."

Khalia was a little surprised, but the plain fact was that she was worn to the bone from the trek and the idea was a welcome one. When Charrisa had helped her to don the gown, she climbed into the bed gratefully and slept until Charrisa woke her to dress for dinner.

Damien met her at the foot of the stairs. Dismissing Charrisa, he escorted her to the dining room. Nigel was no where in sight. Thinking he must be delayed in arriving, Khalia didn't comment on it as Damien helped her into her seat at the table. She realized then that the table was only set for two. It seemed strange that they would be dining alone.

"You are beautiful this evening, your highness."

Khalia was pleased with the compliment. Charrisa had evidently spent the time while she'd been sleeping cleaning and pressing the clothes that Damien had packed for her. When the servant had awakened her, she'd had an outfit laid out that consisted of and emerald green band that covered her breasts, tying at her shoulder blades and around her throat; a matching swatch of fabric to, mostly, cover her genitals; and a sheer shirt that tied just below her waist on one side. "Cleanliness becomes me," she said jokingly.

He chuckled, but shook his head. "A queen accepts such compliments graciously … and there will be many. Not only are you truly beautiful, but there will be those who try to ingratiate themselves with you."

Khalia sighed, her good humor vanishing. "I'm familiar enough with insincerity and lies, thank you. I appreciate the warning, but it really isn't necessary … Why is your brother not joining us?" she added, to soften the shortness of her retort.

Damien frowned. "We have need of eyes and ears at the court. He has gone to meet with Samala to see what has been discovered since the attempt on your life. My younger brother, Basil will join them later, and bring word."

Khalia frowned, turning her attention to her meal. "Who is Samala?"

"He was your grandfather's chief advisor. He is old now, but still active at court … and his loyalty to your family is unquestionable."

"My grandfather?" Khalia echoed, dismayed. "He must be ancient by now!"

Damien shrugged. "As I said, he is old, but he is still sharp … and he is the only one at court at the moment that I felt it safe to trust. I have no more qualms about his devotion to you that my own."

Khalia's heart skipped a beat, but disappointment followed as the realization sank in that he was speaking in a political sense. Nodding, she focused on her meal. "An advisor and a council member are not the same thing?" she asked after a while, not because she was particularly interested in the workings of the government of Atar, but because she was uncomfortable with the silence.

Damien shook his head. "The members of the council are nobles of Atar who represent the people. They act as a ... balance to the Regent's powers. His advisors are there to keep him informed so that the Regent, or King, can make decisions based upon facts rather than hearsay, or whim."

"So ... this isn't a total monarchy? The ruler is not all powerful?"

Damien flushed. "The council was set up in the time of King Caracus' father. We had felt no need for a council in Queen Shamara's reign. She was a just and benevolent queen. When her son took the throne ... he abused his power. It was ... necessary. As queen, you may disband the council, if it is your wish to do so. The people would not rebel."

"But they would've rebelled if any of the male rulers had tried to disband them, is that what you're saying?"

"Yes."

Khalia thought it over and found it almost amusing. "A queen could be just as stupid, self-centered and abusive to her subjects as a king," she pointed out.

"*You* would not," he said with conviction.

Pleasure welled inside her at the compliment. She'd never been particularly comfortable with compliments, however, and cast around in her mind for another subject.

"This place seems strangely thin of company for such a large holding."

Damien frowned. "This is a secret fortress below ground. It was built during the reign of Imarthia the terrible, son of Queen Shamara. My family has improved and expanded upon it many times since then. It is situated below the fortress that guards Nigel's least significant holding. I had planned to take you to his main seat, but I thought this best ... under the circumstances."

Khalia's brows rose. "There is that much danger ...even here?"

They'd finished their meal. Damien rose and moved behind her chair, pulling it out for her as she stood. "Until we have uncovered the extent of the rebellion … yes," Damien said as he escorted her from the dining room and toward the stairs once more. He stopped at the foot of the stairs and Khalia turned to look at him questioningly. "There is also your personal situation. Until you have chosen a mate, bulls will be drawn to fight for your favor. This will intensify to a dangerous level when you once more approach the time of peak fertility."

Chapter Twelve

Khalia sent him a startled look, feeling blood flash into her cheeks hotly before it receded. "You know very well that I find that offensive. Lower animals might behave in such a way, but it's inconceivable that educated, intelligent beings would behave like… like beasts."

Damien's eyes narrowed. "Perhaps we are not so civilized as those of that other world, but all creation feels the need to spawn … Some perhaps more …intensely than others, but just the same…." He frowned. "There is something … unique in you that I have sensed in no other. It disturbs me. I have wondered if I should yield my position as your guardian to someone less … susceptible to your charms, for I can not think rationally much of the time and I fear … I know my guard suffers for it."

There could be no doubt of what he was referring to and still she was reluctant to speak of it. She didn't want him to abandon her to someone else's care, however. "I'm not so sure that would be helpful …leaving someone else to protect me …," she said slowly, feeling her face redden once more.

He frowned thoughtfully. "I'll admit I'm reluctant to do so." He smiled wryly. "But my judgment can not be trusted with you."

Khalia studied him uncomfortably for several moments and finally took the plunge. "I don't know if you really can tell, but my cycle has started again."

He stared at her blankly. "Cycle?"

Khalia sighed. "I *told* you I …we didn't come in season. My cycles are monthly … every month … every twenty eight days it begins all over again."

Damien looked appalled. "This is not possible," he said slowly.

"It *is* possible. It is true. Why would I make up something like that?"

"I thought I had imagined it." He shook his head. "This complicates matters dangerously. It multiplies the chances of detection of our movements tremendously."

After a moment, he lifted her hand and saluted the back of it. "Sleep, sheashona. I will give some thought to what must be done to protect you."

Khalia watched him stride across the hall and shut himself into a room across from the dining room. Finally, she turned and ascended the stairs. Charrisa was waiting for her in the room and Khalia allowed the woman to help her ready herself for bed and dismissed her.

Late as it was, she found she wasn't tired, no doubt because of the nap she'd taken earlier.

It wasn't entirely because of the nap, however, and she knew it. The truth was, it hadn't taken more than the one incident to convince Khalia that the males of this world had a sixth sense when it came to the female reproductive cycle. Despite her nasty remarks about their animalistic behavior, she knew the dragon folk were at the mercy of instincts developed specifically for their species. For whatever reason--probably the longevity of the species--they had limited opportunity to reproduce and it was understandable that their mating practices would reflect that in the intensity of the hunt and the ferocity of competition between the males for fertile females, particularly since it seemed there were far more male than female offspring. From the things that Damien had told her, that seemed indisputable, despite the fact that she'd had little opportunity to observe it for herself.

She wasn't angry and disgusted so much as she was hurt. She'd always considered herself a modern, independent woman. She'd felt no burning need to find a husband in her old life. She thought she might have been perfectly content to remain a spinster, until or unless she found a man who had the ability to change her mind. She certainly wouldn't have considered marrying merely to prove her attraction to the opposite sex ... or because it was expected.

Damien had changed her mind. As often as he irritated her, she couldn't imagine being with anyone else or wanting to. *She* was not a slave to her instincts.

The problem was, he was so resistant to the notion of choosing her that she couldn't help but feel that the *only* thing that drew him to her at all was the instincts he had so much trouble controlling. She wanted more than that. She wanted the sort of bond that she'd sensed between him and his brother, unconditional love. The fact that she'd never had it, in any form, made it all the more desirable.

Despite her strong sense of independence, she had never had any respect for the wild young women who called themselves flappers and no desire to follow in their footsteps. She'd always considered that her morals were above reproach, but she knew better now. Even knowing she would never be completely satisfied with less than everything, she would be perfectly willing to accept Damien as her lover if that was all he was willing, or able, to give her.

The problem lay in convincing him.

And then there was the other little drawback. She was not a seductress. She had virtually no experience with men at all, and none at all in trying to entice a man. Her experience was limited to rebuffing unwanted advances. If strolling around one daily the next thing to naked didn't push a man over the edge, exactly what would it take to do so?

* * * *

Damien paced the study restlessly, trying to cool the fire in his mind sufficiently to think clearly. As often as he had faced the temptation of seducing Khalia into taking him as her lover, he had managed to fight the lure with the certainty that it would be the death of him. In his heart, he knew he would never be able to give her up once he had taken that step, and he also knew he would have no choice once she became queen and selected her mate.

As time wore on, that last thread of sanity had worn thinner and thinner and presented less of a deterrent. For days, he had been wavering, knowing that the longer he stayed with her the greater the chance that he would reach the point where nothing else mattered but having her.

Now that he knew of the threat to her, he'd begun to see it as his duty to protect her and he couldn't decide whether it was actually a logical conclusion or if the knowledge had so neatly aligned with his desire that it had succeeded in pushing him over the edge into insanity.

Once he had marked her as his own, though, he knew few would challenge his possession. There would no longer be the danger of bulls vying for her attention.

Her assertion that this was a monthly occurrence made it all the more dangerous … for both them … for her if he did not take her … for him if he did and succeeded in siring a child on her.

He could have been more comfortable with his conclusions if he had been able to put some distance between them so that he could think more clearly. He knew, however, that that wasn't possible. He couldn't leave her unprotected, and leaving the secret fortress would increase the chance that he would be spotted and she would be found by those bent on assuring that the power of the realm remained as it was.

Finally, in desperation, he left the study and descended into the dungeon. It wasn't much of a compromise, but it was all that he could allow himself. He found that even such a little distance helped. After pacing the dungeon like a caged beast for the better part of two days, he realized that, as neatly as need fit with desire, it was no less true and it was not something he could ignore only because he knew it meant almost certain death.

If his queen had sent him into battle, he would not have questioned it. He would have gone even with foreknowledge that his life was forfeit. It was his duty to die for his queen if necessary.

The logic of his conclusions was no more questionable, whatever his personal desires. He must protect her by whatever means necessary. He could not allow her a choice in the matter, or apprise her of the situation and allow her to make the decision. He knew her well enough by now to know that she would not willingly sacrifice him to save herself.

He *would* not allow her to chose another to sacrifice in his place. His loyalty to his future queen did not extend that far.

* * * *

Khalia was furious … and truth be told, more miserable than she could recall being in her life. It was almost as if Damien could read her mind. No sooner had she decided to seduce him than he had promptly locked himself away from her in the dungeon. She'd had no company but her own and Charrisa's for days and she was sick of both.

If she'd had something to do it wouldn't have been so bad, but she was as much a prisoner here as she'd been in the other fortress. Aside from books and needlework, she didn't even have anything to entertain her. She supposed she should have been grateful for that little bit. Charrisa had gone to a great deal of trouble even producing that much to entertain her, sacrificing her own basket of needlework. The books Charrisa had managed to find had been more dull, if possible, even than the needlework. Most of her time had been spent pacing, bathing, eating and sleeping. She'd explored the secret fortress, but that hadn't consumed more than a few hours of her time.

She'd finally come to the conclusion that she was ready to face whatever was in store for her at Caracaren. Nigel's defection to ferret out the conspiracy had neatly removed any possibility of finding an ally willing to take her home. She'd more than half expected that Damien would decide that she was more trouble than she was worth when she admitted that, unlike the females of this world, she was 'in season' all the time. Instead, he'd defected. She was afraid it was just a prelude to a complete defection, that he would hand her over to someone else to guard.

She supposed, if she'd been an optimist, that prospect wouldn't have seemed so grim. There was some possibility that she might be able to convince her next jailer/protector to take her back to the passage to her own world.

She couldn't convince herself of it, unfortunately. She thought it was far more likely that she would find herself in the hands of a lesser man, one not as devoted to queen and country and duty … one who might force her to accept his attentions.

She didn't suffer any illusions that rebuffing would dissuade a dragon male in the heat of mating or that she was physically capable of enforcing her reluctance.

Growing weary of pacing, she moved to the vanity and sat down. Lifting the brush, she raked the tangles from her hair and began braiding it. As she looked up to search the dressing table for something to secure the ends, she saw Damien's reflection in the mirror behind her.

A shock wave went through her. She felt the blood rush from her face only to flood back with a vengeance. Without a word, he lifted the braid from her suddenly lax fingers and began working the locks of hair free while she stared at him mutely, her mind completely chaotic.

He smoothed her hair when he'd finished and finally took her hand, drawing her to her feet. Dry mouthed, Khalia watched as he lifted her hand to his lips, placing a kiss on the back and then turning it over and pressing his lips to her palm. A tingle of sensation vibrated along her arm as she felt the warmth of his mouth on the sensitive flesh of her palm.

When he lifted his head once more, he merely stared at her, as if waiting. Confused, hesitant, Khalia lifted her free hand to his cheek, stroking her fingers over it. He was clean shaven, but there lingered a very faint roughness of stubble from his beard. The contrast intrigued her.

Truth be told, everything about him fascinated her. He was a study in contrasts. Even in his human form, he had the strength of three men, and yet he was amazingly gentle. He was capable of behaving with purely animalistic savagery one moment and like the most refined of gentlemen the next. He was handsome enough to be a young god, perfect enough to make her acutely conscious of every tiny flaw she possessed. Yet he had a way of looking at her that made her feel like the most beautiful, desirable woman in creation, and if that were not enough, his intelligence and his strong sense of honor and duty commanded absolute faith and respect.

By rights, he should have been pompous, overbearing and conceited. She could have hated him then. Instead, every flaw was balanced with a virtue, and she could neither hate him nor dismiss him as being too good to be true and thus, unbelievable, untrustworthy .. a fraud waiting to be discovered.

He closed his eyes as she explored his cheek and jaw with her fingers, tensing noticeably. Doubt shook her. Had she mistaken his intentions? Had she spent so many nights hoping and dreaming that she'd only imagined his overtures suggested a desire for intimacy? Embarrassment climbed into her cheeks while she tried to think of a way to gracefully withdraw and still save face.

He stopped her when she would have withdrawn. Placing a hand over hers, he held it to his cheek and lifted her other hand to his lips again, then moved up her arm, kissing the pulse point at her elbow before he placed her hand on his shoulder and encircled her waist with his hands, pulling her closer.

Khalia swallowed, staring up at him wide eyed in sudden anxiety, uncertain of how to proceed. She realized she needed to know where she stood, however, and as difficult as it was, she moistened her lips to speak. "You want to be my lover?"

His features tightened. "With every fiber of my being … as long as you, and the gods, will allow," he said huskily.

Disappointment filled her. She'd hoped … but she hadn't really expected anything else and she'd made up her mind that she would accept whatever was offered and try to live with it. She could hardly blame him for having another agenda when she knew that she would leave at the first opportunity.

She surged closer, lifting her face to him, parting her lips in anticipation as weakness washed through her, leaching the strength from her muscles and bones. His breath left him in a rush as he gazed at her, as if he'd been holding his breath, waiting to see what she would do. A gentle quaking traveled through his arms and palms along her waist and into her as he drew her slowly closer, lowering his head until his lips just brushed hers. For many moments, he did nothing more, as if savoring that lightest of touches as he brushed his lips back and forth gently across hers, and then, just as gently, plucked at first her upper lip and then the lower.

Lifting his head fractionally, he drew in a ragged breath, studied her a moment as if waiting for objections and then slid his arms around her tightly, crushing her against his length as his mouth descended once more, this time with hungry urgency held barely in check. Khalia sighed with both pleasure and relief as his mouth covered hers, feeling the rush of dizzying sensation wash through her that she'd felt before when he'd kissed her, and more, the excitement of knowing this time he wouldn't pull away and abandon her with a sense of loss and incompletion.

She dug her fingers into the muscles along his shoulders, then slid her arms around his neck as the heat of his mouth flooded her with a like heat, as his taste and scent and the stroke of his tongue along her own filled her with a hunger for more. Her senses rioted. Heat suffused her. Her racing heart pounded harder still, and faster, until she struggled for breath.

Abruptly, he released her, dragging her arms from around his neck and setting her away from him.

Chapter Thirteen

Stunned, Khalia opened her eyes with an effort, watching numbly as he shrugged his simple garments off and dropped them to the floor. Reaching for her once more, he tugged the ties of her gown loose with fingers that shook noticeably and dragged the sheer fabric off over her head, tossing it aside. He caught her up in his arms when he'd dropped it, carrying her to the bed and laying her gently on top of the coverlet, then tugged his boots off and climbed onto the bed beside her.

Relieved, Khalia turned onto her side and traced her hand slowly down his chest, then along one arm. Her gaze came to rest on the evidence of his arousal and she paused, studying the jutting phallus with a mixture of curiosity and nervousness. It looked impossibly huge. She couldn't imagine how they would fit together, though she knew that they would. Strangely enough the thought of it was enough to dispel the nervousness and replace it with anticipation. Glancing up at him to see if he would object, she reached for him, wrapping her fingers slowly around his erection.

It jerked at her touch and her gaze flew to his face once more. He caught her exploring hand and lifted it to kiss her fingers. "Another time you can explore me as much as you like," he said, his voice rough. "Now is a very bad time."

"Why?" she asked, discovering her own voice was husky.

He ran a hand along her body, stopping to cup one breast and tease the tip with his fingers before he skated his hand along her belly and cupped the mound above her femininity, threading his fingers through the curling hair. "Because I have wanted you so badly, for so long, that I will disgrace myself and disappoint both of us," he growled, leaning toward her and covering the tip of her breast with his mouth and suckling.

A jolt went through her at the contact, snatching the breath from her lungs. She gasped, clutching him to her as he nudged her nipple with his tongue, sending jolt after jolt of exquisite sensation through her. The pleasure was so profound she was of half a mind to drown in it and half a mind to escape the almost unbearable intensity of it. But the moment he ceased tormenting the sensitive tip, lifting his mouth from her, a sense of loss filled her with aching need. Nuzzling the cleft between her breasts, he kissed the edge of each and climbed the second peak, capturing that tip as he had the first, suckling, teasing her to near mindless delight with the tip of his tongue.

When she thought she could bear no more, nor endure it if he ceased, he moved upwards again, placing open mouthed kisses across the upper slope of her breasts, and then her throat. Finally, he sought her mouth once more and kissed her deeply, greedily. She threaded her fingers through his hair, kissing him back with the fervor of her longing, then stroked the silken skin that sheathed his taut muscles along his shoulders and back and finally along his arms and chest and belly.

A tremor went through him. She felt his flesh roughen with tactile sensation as her own had at his touch. Warmth flooded her at his reaction to her touch, and greater need. She moved restlessly beneath him, arching upward to press herself more closely to him, tightening her arms around him.

He resisted the demand, holding himself slightly away from her, stroking her body in a restless caress that awakened every inch of skin that felt the touch of his roughed palm and fingers to heightened sensation. He skated a bare foot along her leg and insinuated one knee between hers. She shifted, spreading her legs to accommodate him, lifting one leg and stoking his hair roughed leg with one foot as his shifted his knee higher until it nudged her femininity.

A jolt went through her at the contact. She moved against his knee, feeling her belly grow taut with need as her breasts had. She began to feel almost fevered with the heat radiating from her body, the dizzying, intoxicating pleasure that filled her mind.

At last, he pulled slightly away from her, holding himself up on one elbow so that he could look down at her. With an effort, she lifted her lids and gazed up at him with complete trust, making no attempt to hide anything that she was feeling. Slowly, he placed a palm over her collar bone and, skimming her body with the lightest of touches, brushed his hand down over her body until his fingers tangled in the curling hair of her woman's mound. He turned to watch the movements of his fingers as he delved her gently, parting the sensitive petals of flesh until he found the heart of her desire. Lifting his gaze to hers once more, he held it as he moved his finger in a tiny, massaging circle that left her gasping for breath, closing her eyes against the intensity of the need she saw in his eyes and felt in her own body. A sense of urgency grew in her as he explored the hot, moist cleft with slow deliberation. She sensed him leaning toward her, felt the heat of his breath a heartbeat before he settled his mouth over hers once more. With a great effort, she lifted her arms, encircling his head as she kissed him back with a sense of desperation and abandon she'd never felt before.

Without breaking his kiss, he moved over her, forcing her thighs apart to accommodate his weight and settling his hips between them. She felt his hand on her thigh, lifting her knee until her foot was planted against the mattress, felt his heated, swollen member slipping along the heated cleft his hand had caressed moments before.

When he broke the kiss and leaned back, she looked up at him, waiting impatiently for what she sensed would come next. She felt him then, the rounded head of his phallus pressing insistently against her, felt the resistance of her flesh, felt her body slowly yielding to his possession as he pressed inexorably into her, claiming her inch by agonizing inch until at last he had buried himself to the root inside of her.

A sense of wonder filled her with the realization that he had joined his body with her own, that she could feel his heated length along her passage, feel the head of his member resting against her womb. She found that she was panting, partly in fear of anticipated pain that never materialized and partly because the need had grown inside of her until she could no longer catch her breath. She looked up at him in mute appeal, knowing he could give her body what it craved, even if she could not name it. "Damien," she said in a throaty gasp of appeal.

His face twisted as it filled with the agony of need denied. Hooking an arm beneath one thigh, he withdrew slowly until he filled only her opening and thrust inside of her again, deeply. Khalia gasped as quakes of pleasure echoed outward from the stroke of his flesh. Digging her fingers into his shoulders, she moved her body in counter to his own as he withdrew slowly again, and again pushed deeply inside of her. A sense of something momentous gathered inside of her with each slow, deep caress until she began to urge him to stroke her faster.

He moved with the demands of her need, watching her face intently as she struggled to reach an unknown goal. Abruptly, the gentle quakes of pleasure gave way to an explosion of ecstasy that tore a ragged cry from her throat as her body convulsed and blackness filled her mind.

Grinding his teeth, he scooped her up into his arms, holding her tightly against him as he sat up, settling on his knees with her astride his lap so that her own weight bore her down upon him, driving him more deeply inside of her. He squeezed her tightly, driving swift and deep and finally shuttering as his own body convulsed in release. "Khalia," he groaned against her throat.

Contentment flooded through her in the aftermath of their lovemaking. At first, she merely clung to him weakly, her head resting on his shoulder, but as her muscles and bones became substantial once more, she kissed the side of his neck and stroked the back of his head.

His arms tightened around her. Finally, holding her to him, he rose up on his knees and moved across the bed. "What are you doing?" Khalia whispered, content with whatever he had in mind, reluctant to lose the feel of his body inside of hers.

Slipping an arm beneath her buttocks, he climbed from the bed. Khalia locked her ankles behind his back as he strode toward the adjoining bath. The faint, musky smell of their lovemaking tickled at her nostrils, but the scent did not offend her, rather the reverse. She nipped his neck playfully as he stepped into the shower with her and finally released her, allowing her to slide slowly down his body. She kissed the faint hollow between his pectorals, and looked up at him dreamily.

His own expression was somber, but the muscles in his face grew taut with renewed need as she gazed up at him. He caught her hair, tipping her head back until he'd exposed the tender flesh of her neck and then lowered his mouth to place a sucking kiss there, climbing up her throat with nibbling bites until her could claim her mouth. The thrust of his tongue inside her mouth sent a wave of heat through her, made her body quicken.

He walked her backwards until her back was pressed against the back wall of the bath and the water pelting from the numerous spouts barely reached them. Lifting her up, he aligned his body with hers once more and drove deeply. Khalia gasped, both startled to feel him erect and hard and driving inside of her, and delighted. She locked her arms and legs around him as he drove into her hard and fast. Instead of building her toward release with the agonizing slowness he had before, he drove her there with swift, savage almost angry thrusts. Within moments she felt the tension seizing her muscles, winding tighter and tighter inside of her.

She knew, now, what her body craved from his, reached out for it, and still it took her by surprise, exploding more powerfully inside of her this time even than before, dragging a startled, ragged cry from her throat. As if her release pushed him over the edge, he released a hoarse, ragged groan, shuddering as he embedded himself deeply.

The release left them both gasping, leaning weakly against the wall. Slowly, he withdrew from her, releasing her to slide down until her feet touched the floor of the bath. Slowly, the strength returned to her muscles and still they trembled as he finally stepped away from her.

Without a word, he lathered a cloth and began to wash her. She stood perfectly still, studying his face surreptitiously, allowing him to do as he would. When he would've rinsed the cloth, she took it from him and bathed

him as he had her. He seemed reluctant to allow it, but he
didn't resist, standing perfectly still as she scrubbed the
cloth over him with the same thoroughness that he had
bathed her.

When they'd rinsed the soap from themselves, Damien
stepped from the bath and grabbed a towel, drying himself
cursorily before he helped her from the tub and dried her.
He retrieved her gown when they had returned to the bed
room, helping her to don it once more and tying the ties at
the sides.

Khalia frowned, feeling the rosy glow that had lingered
from their lovemaking slowly fade at his continued silence,
realizing finally that he meant to leave her. Hurt washed
through her, and behind that anger. "You're not staying."

He glanced at her a moment and then looked away. "If
you wish it," he finally said slowly.

She felt a sudden urge to curse him. Instead, she
swallowed her pride and nodded, reminding herself that she
had decided to take what she could. He lay stiffly beside
her when they'd lain on the bed once more, but when she
turned onto her side and snuggled closely against him, he
stroked her back with a gentleness that made her feel like
crying for some reason she couldn't fathom.

Finally, despite her distress, the repletion of her body
gained the upper hand and she began to drift toward sleep.
"There's always tomorrow," she murmured her thought
aloud.

His arms tightened around her briefly and he leaned
toward her and kissed her brow. "There is no tomorrow for
us, Khalia," he whispered, so faintly she thought she might
have dreamed it. "May the gods have mercy on us both if I
have planted my seed inside of you."

He was gone when she woke. She lay staring at the
ceiling as she listened to Charrisa moving about the room,
wondering if she had dreamed all of it. The faintest
movement of her body was enough to convince her that she
had not … not all of it, at any rate.

His behavior confused her, angered her. When she had
pondered it a while, however, it occurred to her to wonder

if she was misjudging him. He'd guarded her since she had arrived and he had taken the utmost care to treat her in a gentlemanly manner. Perhaps he wasn't reluctant to be with her so much as he was reluctant to blacken her reputation?

She felt better when the thought occurred to her, but she examined it suspiciously, wondering if she'd invented it only to make herself feel better. There was no one, after all, to talk other than the servant, Charrisa ... but then that was probably enough. She wasn't accustomed to having servants, but she'd heard them chattering in the markets of the city. Whatever their employers did seemed highly entertaining to them, and the more damning the tale, the more excited they were to share it.

He cared enough, at least, to make certain she didn't suffer the stigma attached to women of loose morals. It wasn't much, perhaps, especially considering his overdeveloped sense of honor and duty, but it was something.

Feeling slightly better, she got up and dressed and ate her breakfast, then wandered from the room to find him. As she'd more than half expected, he was politely, coolly distant, but she could feel his gaze upon her and when she glanced at him, she caught the heat of his gaze before he looked away. Satisfied, at least for the moment, she allowed him to lock himself away in the study and retired to the apartment she'd been given, biding her time until the evening.

He didn't disappoint her. Charrisa had scarcely left her for the night when he came to her, ravishing her with his urgency, making love to her until she fell into an exhausted sleep.

By the third day, she'd tired of the game and decided to take matters into her own hands. Damien might not be able to think beyond her role as his future queen, but she had not been born to such a role. It was absurd to consider herself above him, beyond his reach. He was a noble. If he cared for her, she had no intention of honoring their silly customs.

Unfortunately, she couldn't be entirely certain that he did care for her … not as a woman, a person. She made up her mind, however, that she would find out, one way or another. If he did not, then she would try to be content with the bargain she had made with her conscience. If he did, then she would not allow anyone in this world to dictate to her whom she should love, and whom she could not.

Her resolve faltered as she descended the stairs, however. There was an ominous quiet about the fortress that she had not sensed before. She tried to dismiss it. With only the three of them staying in the great structure, they rattled about like three peas in a pail. It was always quiet.

She realized the moment Charrisa showed her into the study that she hadn't imagined it. Something was very wrong. Both Damien and the stranger who stood with him made an effort to appear relaxed, but there was strain on both faces and neither man would meet her gaze for more than a moment.

Khalia felt her stomach clench, but since they were making the effort to appear at ease, she followed their lead. "I see we have a visitor?" she remarked questioningly.

Both men knelt, saluting her. When he rose, Damien bowed his head. "Your highness. This is my youngest brother, Basil. He has brought word today from the palace at Caracaren."

With an effort, Khalia smiled, acknowledging the introduction as she studied the newcomer. He was quite as handsome as Damien, in a more boyish manner, though he did not look to be younger by much. There were lines at the corners of his eyes and mouth that spoke of ready smiles and laughter, but no sign now of the happy-go-lucky nature she sensed in him.

She clasped her hands together, feeling the moisture of nerves in her palms. "What word has he brought?"

Damien's face, if possible, looked even more grim. "Both Nigel and Samala have been arrested for plotting treason against you. They are to be tried in two days time … and executed as traitors within the week."

Chapter Fourteen

Khalia merely stared at Damien in shock, her thoughts chaotic as a coldness swept over her. "How civilized of them to try them first," she said faintly. Her lips felt stiff and uncooperative, making it difficult to form the words. She looked around a little vaguely for a place to sit, certain that she would fall if she didn't.

Damien and Basil exchanged a look at her comment, but when Damien glanced at her again a look of alarm washed over his features. Surging forward, he caught her arm and helped her to a chair.

She looked up at him, squeezing his hand gratefully. "So … he's being used as a scapegoat,"

"Yes," he said tightly, turning to pace the room. "I should not have involved them in this."

Khalia stared at him, feeling his pain. Finally, she shook her head. "You are not responsible for what others do, even when you've asked them to do it. They are both grown men, and obviously have been at court long enough to understand the possible consequences--probably better than you. What are we going to do? We have to do something."

"I could go and testify on their behalf," Damien said slowly. "It was I who set them on the errand."

Khalia felt the blood leave her face. For several moments, she thought she might faint. "If they've already planned their execution, I can't imagine that would help them much … besides which, they're liable to decide you're a coconspirator and execute you beside them."

Again Damien and Basil exchanged a look.

"They have already named Damien as one of the conspirators, your highness," Basil said. "They claim that he has slain you and escaped."

"Are you mad, Damien!" Khalia demanded angrily, jumping up from her chair.

"On the surface, I know it must seem so … but I am not without friends at court. If I go, I can explain what has happened and there is a chance that they will listen. My men will support my claims."

"And there is a better chance that they won't! You and I both know the conspiracy is there. You will only succeed in neatly tying things up for them."

Basil smiled wryly. "I have told him this myself, but he is stubborn … And, perhaps he is right. He is well liked by his men, and respected and liked by many at court."

Khalia shook her head. "I won't hear of it. I won't! You will have to take me there. It's the only way to prove you've done nothing wrong. I'll say I was in communication with Samala personally, and that I asked him to discover who had hired the assassins."

Damien's lips thinned. "I would gladly give my life for you, your highness, but I will not take you to your assassins."

Khalia gaped at him for several moments and finally turned to Basil. "Can he do that? Isn't he supposed to do what I say? Isn't that … insubordination or something?"

Basil's eyes gleamed with a touch of amusement. "You can have him thrown in prison for disobeying, your highness."

Khalia looked Damien over speculatively, trying to imagine how many men it would take to subdue him if he decided to resist. "By whom? Do I have an army I don't know about?" she asked dryly.

Basil and Damien exchanged a look. "She has a point. We could raise the army," Basil said.

"We would be risking a war that could tear the realm apart."

"Then I will go. I haven't been accused … yet."

Khalia stared at Basil. "You are as mad as your brother! They will accuse you as quickly as they would him. Even *I* can see that you and your brother are close and I barely know you. They'll never believe that you're not involved if they think that Damien and Nigel are."

"It's the only option we have at the moment ... unless we do nothing at all. You are right about Samala and Nigel. They were well aware of the risks. They were willing to try because they are loyal to you and your family."

Khalia stared at him. "So ... you're suggesting we do nothing and allow those monsters to execute them even though we know, and they know, that they're innocent? How can I live with that? How can you?"

Damien began pacing once more. "In all honesty, your highness, we are powerless at this moment. Until you are crowned, you will be at their mercy, vulnerable to their attacks. The conspiracy is at the highest levels of the government."

"My uncle, you mean?"

Damien frowned. "Possibly, but I am not convinced that he knows anything about it. More likely it is his advisors, or at least one of them, who have governed for many years and now fear to lose their power."

"Why are you so certain it isn't him? Because he doesn't seem interested in anything but his pleasure? That's absurd. In the first place, betrayal runs in the family--if it's true that my uncle kidnapped my grandmother and killed my grandfather. He doesn't know me at all and has no reason to care any more about me than he would any stranger. And he's enjoyed being regent. You said so yourself. He's got as much or more to lose than anybody else."

"All the more reason not to take you to him," Damien pointed out.

Khalia plunked her hands on her hips. "Well, if you're not going to then you might as well take me home! *Then* there'll be no reason for any of this."

Basil looked startled. "You can not mean to abandon your people, your highness! We need the rightful queen upon the throne!"

"You think it's better for me to stay while everybody tries to kill everybody over who's going to rule Atar?"

Again the men exchanged a look. Khalia stamped her foot furiously. "I did not ask for this or want it. You say it is my duty, my birthright. If that's true, and I must stay regardless of my own wishes, then I *will* be queen and I will not be told what I may or may not do! Summon the army of Atar! They will escort us to Caracaren and there will be no war. The conspirators are cowards or they would not sneak about like thieves in the night. They won't openly oppose me … and when we are there, we will discover who the traitors are."

Damien's eyes gleamed with both amusement and, surprisingly, respect. After a long moment, he bowed. "It will be done, your highness."

Shaken, Khalia left the room and hurried back upstairs. She spent the remainder of the day there, more terrified than she could ever remember being in her life. She was not afraid for herself, however. She was afraid for Damien and his brothers.

Would the army support her claim to the throne, she wondered, or had she just demanded something that would end in their downfall?

Was there anything else she could have done? She could think of nothing. As unwilling as Damien was to summon the army and risk a war, he would never have agreed to take her with him otherwise.

He did not come to her that night. She wasn't certain if it was because he and Basil had left to gather the army, or if he'd simply felt it unfitting … or her 'queenly' behavior had driven a wedge between them.

Charrisa woke her the following morning moving about the bedroom far more clumsily than she generally did. When Khalia sat up to look at the woman questioningly, she saw that the woman was as pale as death and obviously terrified. She sank to the floor when she saw Khalia watching her, more as if her knees had given out than pure civility. "Your highness … your army awaits."

At that pronouncement, Khalia felt her heart stop in her chest. It took an effort to retain even the appearance of calm. Finally, she merely nodded and rose, allowing Charrisa to help her to dress.

When they'd completed her toilet, Khalia left the room on shaky legs and went to the stairs, pausing at the top. Below her there seemed a virtual sea of soldiers. Damien was the first to notice her. He knelt. Around him the other men knelt, as well. She recognized the captain of the guard among them, Captain Swiftwing. Nodding at them, she descended slowly, gripping the railing tightly to keep from tumbling to the bottom if her knees gave way.

She realized as she made her descent that there were no more than a handful of men besides Damien and Basil. Doubt shook her, but she did her best to hide it. When she reached the bottom step, she paused. Almost as one, the men looked up at her. "Your highness, Princess Khalia. I pledge my sword and my body to your cause," the men said almost in unison.

Relief trickled through her, but not much. It was hardly an army before her and she looked at Damien questioningly, wondering if the handful of men were all that he and Basil had been able to find willing to support her. He frowned, shaking his head ever so slightly and offered his arm.

She laid her hand upon it and allowed him to lead her where he would. She saw quickly enough that they were leaving the fortress. The garshon had been chained, but as they reached the dungeon, it howled and snarled and fought the chains that held it. A shiver skated over her. Apparently sensing her uneasiness, Damien laid a hand over hers, squeezing it reassuringly as they made their way down the passage that led to the secret entrance.

The sunlight dazzled her when she emerged at last. She blinked, trying to adjust her vision to the brightness. When her vision focused at last, she had to stifle the urge to gasp. In the fields below them, as far as the eye could see in any direction, lay an army of dragon men.

Khalia glanced uncertainly at Damien as he released her arm and stepped back, kneeling as all the men around her knelt. She glanced around at the sea of men, feeling her fear slowly evaporate. Something strangely akin to pride filled her as she studied them. She stepped forward, raising her voice to be heard. "I am Khalia, daughter of Princess Rheaia. Will you accept me as your queen?"

To her surprise and faint embarrassment, she heard her voice echo outward, flowing into the distance. For a moment that seemed frozen in time, only the wind answered. Then, like an echo returning to her, she heard the shout from thousands of throats. "Queen Khalia!"

When the shouts died down at last, she spoke again. "Then let us go to Caracaren!"

They rose to their feet, shifting, and where before there had been an army of men, an army of dragon men stood in their place. She closed her eyes as she felt Damien's arms close around her, lifting her against his scaly chest, a sense of warmth and peace flowing through her as the rustle of thousands of flapping wings filled the air, stirring it to a whirlwind as the army rose into the sky. She would've been content merely to rest against him and feel the warmth and power of his great body.

"You have done well, my sheashona," Damien said low, his voice gravelly and rumbling from his chest.

She opened her eyes and looked up at him, smiling faintly in pleasure before the reality of their situation flooded back. Her smile faltered. "In time, we will see."

He shook his great head. "The blood of royalty flows through your veins, Princess. If I had ever doubted it, I would doubt it no longer. *This* you were born for. Whatever the future brings, I will never regret pledging my loyalty to you."

Khalia looked away, resting her cheek against his chest as his words evoked a dim memory. *There is no tomorrow for us, Khalia.*

A shiver of uneasiness went through her. Was this what he'd meant, she wondered? That they would be forced to fight for the crown he was so determined to place upon her head? That many would die to see it settled there? Perhaps even him?

She pushed it from her mind, unwilling to dwell on it, or the sense of injustice that filled her that she was the unwilling altar upon which so much blood might be spilled.

The sun was low on the horizon by the time she saw the city she knew must be Caracaren. Even from a great distance, she could see it looked like nothing from the world she'd come from. Like a dish sent spinning into the sky, it hovered above the ground as if the clouds beneath it supported it. Tall buildings reached upward like pointing fingers, far taller than anything she had ever seen and all were linked by strange, clear tubes. As they came nearer, she could see dark objects shooting through the tubes. It reminded her of the pod Damien had taken her in to escape the fortress, though these seemed bigger, and longer.

"What are those ropy looking things?" she whispered to Damien curiously.

He glanced down at her. "Transportation for the people of the city."

Like streetcars? She didn't pursue it, however. She doubted if he would understand streetcars any more than she understood these things.

As they drew nearer, she began to see people running in the streets or huddled together in frightened knots. The army formed into a narrow line behind them as they descended and began to fly between the neat rows of towering buildings. Finally, ahead of them, she saw an enormous plaza. A single, enormous building surrounded it. People poured through the great front doors, some soldiers, some obviously civilians, and lined up on the tiered steps that led up to the great doors from the plaza below.

Damien settled to the concrete plaza with a slight jolt and set Khalia on her feet. She glanced back at him. He remained in his fearsome dragon form. Glancing around, she saw that the army that had settled around them followed his lead. Abruptly, a commotion at the entrance to the palace drew her attention once more. A stout man of no more than medium height was making his way down the stairs, his bearing regal despite the indulgence that had gathered at his middle.

"What is the meaning of this?" he demanded imperiously, when he'd looked out over the army.

Damien inclined his head. "As you see, your highness, we have brought our future queen for her coronation."

The man reddened, but a smile suddenly lit his face as he hurried forward. It wasn't until he neared her that Khalia saw that the smile was obviously forced. He spread his arms wide, as if in welcome. "My niece! Your are the image of your dear mother!" he said loudly, making certain everyone within three yards of them heard the 'joyous' reunion between the niece and her great uncle--Maurkis, brother of King Caracus.

She knew in that moment that he was behind the conspiracy to kill her and a wave of nausea washed through her. Nevertheless, she allowed him to embrace her, even returned his embrace, doing her best to appear at least as sincere as he was.

When he drew back, she forced a smile. "We have come to see to it that my loyal men, Nigel Bloodragon and Samala Greystreak are released. They were unjustly charged and imprisoned," she said loudly enough that everyone near them could hear.

His face darkened, but his smile remained firmly in place. "We will not talk politics just yet … especially when you have not had the time to be fully informed about the charges."

She gave up the effort to keep her smile in place. "I am completely informed. I sent them here …mistakenly thinking the conspiracy was here, in the palace. General Bloodragon has discovered, however, that the plot was hatched by our enemies, the Baklen to start a war," she lied, turning and speaking more loudly.

Something flickered in Maurkis' eyes and was quickly hidden. "But … this is wonderful news! Our good friends must be released at once!" He turned from her, issuing the order to the men nearest him. When he turned to look at Khalia again, his smile was firmly in place once more. He offered his arm. After a moment, Khalia laid her fingers on it and allowed him to escort her up the stairs into the palace. "Our enemies, you say? We will put our heads together and think of a fitting punishment for the enemies of Atar, who would dare to harm our future queen."

She glanced back at Damien and saw that he had shifted from beast to man. Of a certainty, he thought the danger past or he would not have done so. She smiled. "I will depend upon you, General Bloodragon, to keep me informed."

He nodded, bowing, but he either did not catch the subtle suggestion that she expected to see him or there were matters that prevented it. A full week passed before she saw him again.

Chapter Fifteen

There were degrees of boredom, Khalia discovered. In all the time that she'd been in this strange world, she hadn't had any of the work that usually filled her days, and yet, she had not truly been bored until she was faced with the regimen set up for her once she reached the palace.

She was to be crowned within the month and preparations had to be made; decisions on the feast, the entertainment the celebrations before, during and after, the coronation itself. She had to have a wardrobe. She had to have lessons in etiquette and diplomacy. She had to sit in on sessions of the court with her council to learn the workings of the government.

She would have preferred her books and studies for the museum, or sitting quietly with her needlework.

She would have preferred dining alone with Damien, or slogging through swamp water, teasing him, snuggling next to him in a crude hut on a bed of grasses.

She hated being surrounded by throngs of people day in and day out. It reminded her far too forcibly of her life in the orphanage where privacy had not even been a concept to her. Even in her own apartments, people came and went and giggled and talked until she felt as if she was living in a department store window, always watched, always on display.

It was far too much like the life in the orphanage she'd
hated, where she'd felt like no one considered her an
individual or even a human being, but rather more like a
farm animal that was herded from bath, to dining hall, to
chores, to bed in an endless round, where the only time
anyone actually looked at her and saw her was when she
misbehaved and was singled out for punishment. The only
difference that she could see was that now she was the only
cow and a herd had been sent to attend her.

She bore with it because she had no choice, because lives
depended upon her assuming the role as queen of a world
she still couldn't think of as her own. She bore with it
because Damien expected no less of her and she couldn't
bear to disappoint him.

When he didn't come to her, even at night when she shut
everyone out and lay in her bed alone, she began to wonder
why she put up with it at all. She had power now. She
could go home. No one truly wanted her. No one would
suffer for her absence, least of all the uncle that smiled at
her and doted upon her and wished her dead with every
glance.

However, the painful truth was that she was as much a
captive as she'd been from the first, maybe more so now,
for there was not one moment, waking or sleeping, that
guards and servants and advisors and councilors didn't
surround her.

About a week after her arrival at the palace, she sensed a
stir of excitement in the women who'd been assigned to
care for her. They seemed more bubbly than usual as they
went through her wardrobe, searching for the perfect outfit
for her to wear to the state dinner that she was to attend.
Khalia watched them in the mirror as she sat before her
dressing table, enduring a session with the woman whose
only duty seemed to be in dressing her hair--a complete
absurdity in her book. She was a 'maiden'. Maidens wore
their hair loose about their shoulders--period. Once she was
mated, she would be allowed to wear her hair coiled and
pinned in elaborate styles, but not now.

For the first time in her life, she'd been tempted to emulate the flappers and hack her 'crowning glory' off at her shoulders.

When the maid had finished combing and curling her hair, she began to carefully weave bejeweled ribbons through it. Finally, she produced an elaborate headdress and settled the heavy piece on top of Khalia's head, pinning it in place with dozens of gouging hair pins that almost instantly produced a headache.

She discovered when she went to rise from the bench at last that the thing had to be carefully balanced. She had to stand perfectly straight and she could not move her head more than a few degrees in any direction. Briefly, rebellion rose inside of her and she was tempted to rip it from her head and fling it across the room.

She quelled it. She had not been reared to become queen and there was much to be learned regarding appropriate behavior, but she *had* grown up in an orphanage and she was well versed in the need for conformity.

She discovered the outfit her handmaidens had chosen was equally beautiful and just as torturous to wear. The top was fairly typical in design--nothing more than two tiny wedges of fabric to cup her breasts and strung together by narrow ties that went around her neck and her back. It differed only in that it was so encrusted with jewels that it was stiff and abrasive to her skin.

The bottom was as bad or worse. The hair on her mound had been shaved to no more than a tiny strip... and that was barely covered by the scrap of bejeweled cloth. The tiny triangle narrowed between her legs and became not much more than a string in the back, which tucked between the cheeks of her buttocks in back, leaving both buttocks completely bare. Some sadistic bastard had had the bright idea of stringing jewels even along the narrow ties, however, and the tiny, sharp stones immediately became a painful reminder of just how sensitive that area was.

She sincerely hoped she wouldn't be expected to dance in the thing.

The maids had chosen a sheer blue skirt to tie about her waist. It snagged immediately on the jeweled femi-piece she wore, however, and Khalia found she lacked the patience to deal with that irritation on top of the headdress and the discomfort of the bejeweled femi-piece and top. "No," she said emphatically, removing the skirt and tossing it aside.

Her maids stared at her. "But… your highness. It would be … shockingly disgraceful to appear in public without a skirt!"

Khalia looked at the woman hard, trying to decide if she was joking or not. She appeared to be completely serious. "I'm next door to naked now!" she said indignantly. "You're saying this is all right, so long as I wear a 'veil' over it that's thin enough I could read through it?"

The women exchanged uncomfortable glances. "It is the custom."

Khalia's eyes narrowed. "I've no intention of worrying with that thing catching every time I take a step, or breathe. I'll wear it like this, or you can find something else."

The woman who'd spoken before bit her lower lip and looked at the other women for support. When no one said anything, she bowed her head. "Your highness, we were ordered to dress you in your finest garments. You have nothing richer."

Khalia shrugged. She hadn't really expected them to produce anything else. "Then I suppose I will set a new style tonight."

They stared at her, some obviously frightened, others shocked, some just as obviously fighting a desire to giggle. She ignored all of them. The gigglers giggled at everything--she meant to rid herself of them at the first opportunity. The women who disapproved, seemed to disapprove of everything she did.

The maid who'd dressed her hair came forward timidly, carrying a deep blue length of the thickest material Khalia had seen since she'd arrived. "This robe was intended for after your coronation, your highness, but it is heavy fabric, unlikely to snag on the jewels as the other does."

"She is not to wear that until she is queen. It is a robe of office."

Khalia looked at the woman. "What office?"

"A robe of state, your highness," the woman stammered. "When you are queen."

Khalia drew a long suffering sigh and glanced at her hairdresser. "I'll wear the robe," she said firmly, more from sheer contrariness than any real desire to wear it. Moving to the bench she'd just vacated, she sat while the hairdresser attached a stiff contraption across her shoulders and around each arm to support the robe, secured the robe and then very carefully arranged her hair again.

When she stood once more, she saw that nearly half the handmaidens had vanished. The others were cowering in the corners. She glanced at her hairdresser and shook her head slightly. "Timid little mice."

The hairdresser fought a smile, but became serious almost at once. "It is not the acceptable mode of dress at court, your highness, but they should not presume to tell you what you may, or may not, wear."

"Exactly," Khalia said. "What are you called?"

"Guiteanna ... daughter of General Fireater."

Khalia frowned thoughtfully and finally placed the name. The girl's father was a lesser noble, who had distinguished himself in the last war and been promoted to general ... Much as Damien had, except that Damien had still been a very young man and had risen much faster and higher in rank. "Thank you, Guiteanna."

The silence that fell over the state dining room when she was announced might have alarmed her, or embarrassed the person that she had been. Contrarily, it sent a ripple of grim satisfaction through her. She'd been a conformist all of her life, and it had only secured her position as a nonentity, a ghost among the living who was accounted as nothing and ignored.

If the only satisfaction open to her was in defying their traditions, then she would enjoy what she could.

Smiling faintly, she descended the short flight of stairs. As if her movement had finally shaken them from their shocked immobilization, the assembly scrambled to recover themselves, bowing deeply.

She was escorted to the seat her uncle had occupied at every other function she'd attended. Surprise flickered through her, but she took the seat. Her uncle was red with fury when he took his seat beside her. She gave him a cool look.

"Your highness," he muttered under his breath. "I have not officially stepped down. Until your coronation …people will talk."

She lifted her brows at him. "What will they say?"

She hadn't thought it possible he could turn any redder. He proved her wrong. "It is insulting," he said in a hissing voice.

"Why would you feel slighted? You told me you were anxious to 'hand the weighty mantle of office to me', that you were 'weary of carrying it'."

Maurkis looked for several moments as if he would strangle, or die of a seizure. Finally, he merely nodded and sat back as a servant arrived to place the first course before them.

Khalia let out a surreptitious sigh of relief. It hadn't been her intention to challenge Maurkis openly, particularly when she knew he must still be plotting against her and doing so was liable to bring him into the open, as well, or drive him to more desperate measures. On another level, she didn't regret it. She had disliked him on sight, because she had sensed that he was weak, self-indulgent, greedy, suffered from an inflated opinion of himself, and stupid. Nothing she'd discovered since had led her to change her opinion of him.

Ignoring him, she glanced down the table as the other diners finally began settling in their seats. Her heart skipped a beat when she caught a glimpse of a man far down the table. The woman blocking her view finally turned her head away, flirting with the man on her other side, and Khalia realized that it wasn't merely hopefulness. It was Damien.

For a long moment, their gazes met down the length of the table. Finally, he inclined his head and returned his attention to his diner partner.

In that single moment, he completely annihilated her composure and her self-confidence. With an effort, she focused on her meal, allowing the chatter around her to wash over her while she wrestled with her chaotic thoughts and emotions. It was something Maurkis said during the fourth course that finally penetrated her abstraction. She glanced at him and saw a complacent smile was curling his lips. "I'm sorry. What did you ask?"

Amusement flickered in his eyes. It was purely malicious, however, and Khalia knew even before he repeated his question that it would be something she would find very unpleasant. "The petitioners. Have you reviewed them yet?"

Khalia searched her mind for what he was referring to. Vaguely, she recalled that one of the ministers had given her a stack of papers to look over earlier, but she'd been so distracted by the commotion her maids created in her suite that she had merely set them aside.

"Not yet."

His brows rose. He slid a glance down the table toward Damien, watching him for several moments. Unable to resist, Khalia followed his gaze. The women seated on either side of him were vying for his attention and a wave of jealousy washed over her. The moment she met her uncle's gaze again, she realized she'd given herself away.

"I'm surprised you haven't looked at them yet. You'll be expected to settle upon one very quickly … preferably before the coronation."

She hadn't a clue of what he was talking about, but she had no intention of allowing him to know it. She could either contain her curiosity until she retired to her apartment where she could look at the papers, or she could wait for him to gloat over it … whatever 'it' was.

"Perhaps this diner will prove enlightening, however. It will give you the opportunity to meet some of the men who have petitioned for your hand, and then you may look through the petitions and match faces to the reports."

Despite everything that she could do, Khalia could not prevent the shock wave that went through her, or the nausea that followed it. She supposed she had known that this would be a part of what was expected of her, but none of it had ever seemed real to her. She'd continued to nurse a forlorn hope that she would somehow escape and return to her old life in her own world. And then there had been the deeper fantasy that Damien would rescue her and claim her for his own.

"You never chose a mate," she pointed out finally.

He shrugged. "In my case it was not only not necessary, but frowned upon. I was … am nothing more than regent to hold the throne for the true ruler. It was the will of the people that I not breed heirs that might try to interfere with the succession. You are to be the queen, however. You must produce an heir. Moreover, being a female has the added draw back of your reproductive processes. If you have not settled upon a proper mate beforehand, it is not too farfetched to consider the likelihood of a war breaking out over claiming your favor."

Dimly, she remembered that Damien had said something about that. The truth was, she'd been so inundated with demands since her arrival, and so frightened about the outcome when they'd set out to come, that she'd completely forgotten the very dangerous situation her cycles put her in.

Something had changed, however. Despite the fact that she should have found herself in the midst of battles to claim her by now, the 'bulls' that surrounded her day in and day out hardly gave her more than surreptitiously admiring glances.

She frowned, mentally calculating, but the truth was these creatures were far more knowledgeable about such things than she was. All she knew was that at some point between her courses, she was fertile. She might have been fertile when she and Damien had lain together, and she might not. She could do nothing but wait until the next time she was due to start her courses … and even then she couldn't be completely certain. She was generally as predictable as sunrise, but emotional strain could well interfere and she'd certainly endured a great deal of emotional strain in the past few weeks.

She didn't know why, but it hadn't occurred to her that the males might be able to sense that she'd been claimed. She wondered now if their lack of extreme interest was merely the result of having had intercourse with him. Or did it mean that she was carrying Damien's child?

Chapter Sixteen

Ignoring the gloating expression on Maurkis' face, Khalia concentrated on behaving with indifference to his remarks, making small talk whenever anyone spoke to her and an attempt to show interest in the elaborate dishes set before her. It occurred to her presently, however, that among the last of their conversations, she had finally confessed to Damien that she was not like the females of his world. That she did not come in season. Her cycles were monthly. His response had been that he would give some thought to what he could do to protect her.

Hurt and anger surged through her when she realized, at last, what that solution had been. He'd become her lover.

She thought for some moments that she would not be able to retain a facade of unconcern, but her years in the orphanage came to her rescue once more. She had learned, at a very early age that the surest way to be tormented was to allow the tormentor to see that he'd made his mark.

Sucking in a deep, relaxing breath, she forced all of it to the back of her mind. She could examine it later--if she wanted to--when she had at least a little privacy. She couldn't allow herself to think about it now.

She was relieved when the interminable diner ended at last--until she discovered that it was to be followed by dancing and that she was not to be allowed merely to sit and watch. As her uncle had so gleefully pointed out, many of her suitors were in attendance. It could be potentially dangerous to snub them and retreat to her room like an empty headed, thoughtless child.

She danced with all of them as they were presented to her. The youngest was barely more than a boy, fresh faced, earnest, clumsy and eager to please. The oldest looked to be about her uncle's age. Within a very few minutes with him, she had learned far more than she wanted to; that he had been mated many years earlier, but had lost her to child bearing; that he was brother to the queen of their closest ally; and that he was a lecher of the first order.

Damien danced with virtually every unattached female--except her.

She was relieved when she'd finally worked her way through the list. The moment she did, she excused herself and retired for the evening.

She found as she strode toward her apartments, leaving most of her attendants behind, that she'd reached the limit of her endurance. Standing in the door of her suite, she ordered everyone out. The maids and ladies in waiting merely gaped at her as if she'd lost her mind. She glared at them for several moments and finally stepped outside and looked up at the two guards standing at attention on either side of the entrance to her apartment. "Remove them."

The guards exchanged a glance. Saluting her, they turned and marched into the room, each grabbing two ladies by the arm and escorting them from the room. The others shrieked and fled.

Breathing a sigh of relief, Khalia closed the doors behind them, pulled the elaborate headdress she was wearing from her hair and tossed it aside. The robe followed and behind that the jewelry and the heavily embroidered garments. She wanted nothing so much as to remove the taint of this corrupt, dissolute palace from her ... and to remove herself from it, but a bath would have to suffice.

The trill of birdsong penetrated her abstraction and she glanced at the little sheashona fluttering about the gilded cage in one corner. It was only one of the many gifts that had arrived for her to celebrate her coronation, but it was the only one that had really touched her. Generally, she spent time talking to it, feeding it, watching it flutter about its cage when she retired for the evenings, enjoying it as much because it reminded her of Damien as for its own sake.

Tonight, she wanted no reminders.

Swallowing with an effort, she turned away from it and headed toward her bedchamber.

He stepped out of the shadows near her bed, startling her. She stopped abruptly, her heart hammering uncomfortably in her chest. "Damien? How did you …?"

She saw then that his face was a mask of carefully controlled rage. His eyes glittered with it and with something else that made her heart beat erratically, crushed the air in her lungs so that she had to struggle to breathe.

"I used the passage … the one that links the queen's chamber to that of her consort."

Khalia merely stared at him, trying to make sense of his comments. A passage? She hadn't even known there was one, let alone that she'd been installed in the queen's apartments. It occurred to her after only a moment, however, that there was accusation in his voice and manner. It resurrected the hurt and anger she'd been working so assiduously to subdue.

"Did any pique your interest?"

Khalia's eyes narrowed. "Any what?" she asked tightly.

"Any of the hopeful males vying for your favor."

How could they when she could think of no one but him? "I don't believe that falls under the heading of your business. Unless you're suggesting that we're such great friends we should share our darkest secrets with one another? You go first. Which of the females fondling you tonight gets to share her bed with you?"

She'd been so caught up in her hurt and anger, she hadn't realized that he was stalking her as a cat stalked its prey, moving slowly and unthreateningly closer, inch by inch.

Something flickered in his eyes, but he didn't deny the accusation. "You've changed."

"You changed me," she countered before she even considered the implications, but then the comment had thrown her off guard. It had seemed a suggestion that he was displeased with the changes he sensed in her. It was as grossly unfair and hurtful as everything else he'd done. She knew it was true, though. She was even more distrustful, if possible, than she had been before, harder, angrier with life.

"I tried to stay away," he said after a moment, some of the anger leaving his face.

"You succeeded," she responded tartly. "You've done everything you set out to do, so now you can go." She turned her back on him then, stalking angrily toward the adjoining bath. He caught up to her before she reached it, catching her hand and swinging her around to face him once more. Without thinking, Khalia swung at him with her free hand as he pulled her around. He caught that wrist, as well, forcing her hands behind her back.

She glared at him furiously, fighting the urge to burst into tears. "My guards will be through that door in two seconds if I call out to them."

His lips tightened. "Summon them. I can kill them both in less time that that," he growled.

It wasn't the threat that stopped her or even any doubt that he could do just as he said. It was the certainty that, regardless of everything, she could not bring herself to hurt him in any way. "Why did you come?" she asked a little breathlessly.

Something flickered in his eyes. Slowly his gaze traveled over her face and down her body, like a caress. He swallowed convulsively. "Because I could not stay away," he said harshly, dipping his head toward hers and capturing her lips in a kiss that seared her to her soul. All the longing she'd denied sprang insistently to life and she surged toward him, coming up on her toes to offer him better access, pressing her body longingly against his. The little restraint he'd held onto broke at her first sign of surrender.

Releasing her wrists, he caught her shoulders and surged backward with her until she felt a gentle collision with the wall at her back. He pressed tightly against her, pinning her to the wall with his body as he shrugged his garments off and allowed them to fall where they would.

Freed from restraint, she caressed every part of his body that she could reach, stroking her fingers through his silky hair, then along his shoulders and his back. When she slipped her arms beneath his, however, and stroked his buttocks and thighs, he broke the kiss. "Don't touch me," he growled, grabbing her wrists and manacling them to the wall on either side of her head.

The snarl of barely leashed savagery penetrated the fog of heated desire. Before she could do more than blink at him in surprise, however, he covered her mouth once more in a kiss that made her knees give way, thrusting his tongue possessively into her mouth and raking it along her own. She was gasping for breath when he tore his mouth from hers and dropped his mouth to the curve between her neck and shoulder, sucking so hard the flesh tingled on the edge of pain before he moved lower still, placing a chain of similar burning kisses along the upper slopes of her breasts.

Discovering his hold on her prevented better access, he released her wrists and reached behind her, cupping her buttocks and lifting her up along the wall until her breasts were nearly level with his face. She caught his shoulders, looping her arms around his neck to keep her balance as he captured the peak of one breast in his mouth, ravishing it with his tongue and sending mind shattering waves of intoxicating desire through her. Weakness followed and she felt herself slipping. She wrapped her legs tightly around his waist.

He hoisted her higher, slipping one arm beneath her hips and struggling to align his hard shaft with her body. A shudder went through her as she felt him stroking the sensitive flesh of her cleft. She tightened her arms, wondering a little wildly if he could impale her in such a position, desperate to feel him inside of her.

She gasped as he sank home, squeezing her eyes tightly at the exquisite torture of his slow possession. Her muscles still resisted the immense girth of his member, clinging, impeding his full possession, but her body welcomed him. The moisture of desire drenched her passage. As it grew slick with wanting, gravity provided the last resistance he needed to bury himself deeply.

He withdrew almost at once and thrust deeply again, grinding his pelvis against her to drive deeper still. He battered at her with the mindless precision of a piston engine, growling as he thrust over and over. The same madness welled inside of her as her body rejoiced in the savagery of his possession. A series of tiny explosions erupted inside of her, one after another, finally culminating in a climax that seemed to stop her heart for several moments when she felt his member jerk suddenly and spew his hot seed inside of her.

Trembling in the aftermath, she clung to him weakly, feeling the pounding of his heart against her breasts, listening to his hoarse, ragged breath. Slowly, his body withdrew from hers and he allowed her to slip down until her feet rested on the floor.

He leaned his forehead against the wall above her head, struggling to catch his breath. Finally, he pulled a little away from her. Lifting his hand, he cupped her cheek. "I did not hurt you, sheashona?" he asked hoarsely.

If he'd said anything but that! The endearment was almost her undoing. She shook her head, not trusting herself to speak.

A look of dismay flickered across his features. "I did…."

She placed her fingertips on his lips briefly and shook her head again. "It's just … Nothing."

He frowned. Finally, he scooped her into his arms and carried her to the bed. When he'd settled her, he climbed onto the mattress beside her. Relief flooded her. She'd been afraid that he meant to leave her. Before he could question her further, she rolled onto her side facing him and slipped one arm around his neck. "Make love to me again," she whispered near his ear, tugging on his ear lobe playfully with her teeth.

He needed no further prompting. He made love to her slowly, gently, thoroughly arousing her once more before he moved over her and brought her to glorious culmination as he had that first time.

As they lay basking in the aftermath of their lovemaking, she cuddled close to him and asked about his brother.

He frowned, obviously reluctant to speak.

"Something's happened to him."

He lay back against the pillow, staring up at the ceiling. "They claimed he'd escaped. When we went to release him, he was gone. Samala knew nothing, but he suspects that they took him away … perhaps with the intention of holding him hostage for my behavior. In any case, I've not been able to discover anything …yet."

Khalia swallowed her dismay, wishing she hadn't brought it up after all. "I'm sorry … Do you think he's still alive?"

Damien sighed. "I feel that he is. I just don't know if I can trust my instincts on this one."

"What will you do?"

"There is little that I can do right now, beyond awaiting word either from Nigel that all is well … or from those who hold him demanding something for his return. I have sent out men to search for him, but there is much ground to cover."

There seemed nothing to say to that, beyond offering her sympathy, and she sensed he didn't want that. She lapsed into silence, snuggling close to him, idly stroking his body. She was drifting to sleep when she felt him move away from her and get up. She'd expected that he would leave and she was still disappointed.

Resolutely, she ignored it, feigning sleep. In time, she found it.

Despite her disappointment the night before when Damien had left her, she rose the following morning feeling far more cheerful. She discovered she didn't really want to know why he'd stayed away, or why he'd felt compelled to return. All that mattered was that she had something to look forward to. Knowing he would come to her in the night made everything else more bearable.

She was so happy, so wrapped up in memories of the night before that it wasn't until that evening that she became aware of the fact that her ladies were eyeing her, blatantly suspicious. Uneasiness welled to tamp her enthusiasm. It wouldn't do, she knew, to thrust them into the midst of a scandal virtually on the eve of her coronation. The atmosphere crackled with tension as it was.

Moreover, she'd learned enough to know now that Damien hadn't exaggerated when he'd told her he could not be considered her equal, or even close enough to be considered a suitable candidate as her consort. It was ridiculous, of course, but she supposed, looking at it from their perspective, she could see their point. Except that she didn't believe she was the princess as they supposed.

It presented difficulties that didn't seem to have answers at the moment. She could not claim *not* to be the daughter of Princess Rheaia. It was far too dangerous even to consider such a route, but as long as they believed her to be, they would also consider Damien unsuitable.

Perhaps there would be some way that she could elevate him once she was queen?

Always assuming Damien actually wanted her to.

He was proud. What if he refused to even consider it? He was not mated. She'd managed to learn that much at least. Which mean that he was free to chose, but also made her wonder if there were reasons other than the position she held that he made him reluctant to chose her. Was he too proud to ally himself with a woman when he knew everyone would consider him beneath her?

Or was it, as she'd feared all along, that his feelings for her did not go beyond the instincts he had so much difficulty controlling… and his honor, loyalty and duty to his queen?

Did it matter if she could have him?

It did. It would be torture to feel as she did toward him and know he didn't return those feelings, but surely not nearly as much torture as watching him chose another.

She was afraid she was becoming obsessed with him. No matter how hard she tried to concentrate on other matters, her mind returned to him again and again. She knew, instinctually, that she loved him beyond all reason. It could be nothing but instinct, for she'd never before loved, or even felt the love, of another being. She supposed it was that emptiness waiting to be filled that made her feelings for him so desperate and all consuming, and perhaps it was for the same reason that it had taken her so long to understand it for what it was.

Regardless, it was both joy and torment, bringing fears to light that she'd thought she had long since buried, bringing her a sense of reason for being.

She'd paced the room for hours that night and finally given up the hope that he would come and gone to bed. With the first caress of his hand, her body awoke to his touch, alive and eager for him. Drowsily, she opened her eyes and looked up at him. He was propped on one elbow, studying her. He leaned down to kiss her when he saw that she was awake and looking up at him.

Chapter Seventeen

Khalia lifted her lips to meet him, but placed a hand on his chest, pulling away after only a moment. "You promised that I could explore your body," she whispered, her voice still husky with sleep.

His gaze flickered over her face, but finally he settled back, tucking one arm behind his head, watching her. Khalia raised up on one elbow, stroking her hand over his body. With her first touch, his flesh prickled, his nipples becoming tight and erect. Intrigued, she leaned closer, wondering if his male nipples were as sensitive as her own, and placed a tentative kiss there. She was no wiser when she'd done so. He tensed, but she couldn't tell whether it was purely from her kiss or if her touch there produced

more intense pleasurable sensation than if she'd kissed him
elsewhere.

Dismissing her doubts, she decided there was pleasure
enough in it for her. She'd wanted to caress him and give
him pleasure as he did her. She still did. She just hadn't
realized that she would find it almost as exciting as when
he caressed her.

Coming up on her knees, she leaned over him, supporting
herself on one arm as she stroked his body with her hand,
and followed with her lips. The warmth and tension inside
of her grew with each experimental touch, each kiss. The
scent of his flesh, the taste of it on her lips sent a heady rush
through her. No longer content merely to kiss him, she
flicked her tongue over his skin, sucked little love bites into
her mouth.

She became aware as she made her way down his chest
that it rose and fell more and more rapidly, that his breath
was ragged, his body trembling with the effort to remain
perfectly still as she explored him. That awareness sent a
rush of heat through her, a heady sense of power and
elation that inspired her to explore him with more reckless
abandon. Rising up on one elbow again, she skated her
hand down over his ribs and belly and finally stroked his
phallus. It jerked beneath her touch, startling her and her
gaze flew to his. His eyes were tightly shut, his face
contorted, as if he was in excruciating pain.

She could not have hurt him. She was certain of that, but
undoubtedly she had found the one spot on his body that
was more intensely sensitive than any other. She wrapped
her fingers around it, and slid her hand along it. He let out a
ragged gust of air, tensing all over. A wave of heat prickled
over her skin. Her mouth went dry. Slowly, she leaned
forward to taste him, running her tongue along the length of
his member and then encircling the rounded tip. Finally,
she opened her mouth over his heated flesh.

He caught her hair as she slipped it into her mouth, his
fingers curling, but he made no attempt to thrust her away
and after a moment, she sucked at the rounded head of his
member experimentally. A shudder went through him. He

gasped hoarsely. Her body reacted as if he were kissing her instead of the other way around, her belly clenching, her femininity beginning to pulse with the need to feel his possession.

Closing her eyes, she moved his member in and out of her mouth, sucking him more feverishly as the blood pounded in her head and her body tightened with tension.

Abruptly, he caught her. Pulling her away, he sat up, shoving her back roughly against the pillows. Khalia was still gasping in surprise when he caught her legs and snatched them apart, covering her clit with his mouth. She cried out at his tender assault on the sensitive bud with his tongue and mouth, her heart pounding with a hard rush of such exquisite sensation, her body racing so fast toward culmination she found she couldn't catch her breath.

Mindlessly, she dug her fingers into his hair, tugging, certain she couldn't bear the intensity of the sensations he was evoking with the teasing onslaught of his mouth and tongue. He caught her hands, forcing them to the bed on either side of her hips, and she dug her fingers into the sheets, panting for breath so harshly it became little high pitched cries of ecstasy. He covered her mouth with one hand, reminding her abruptly of the guards outside her door, and she caught his hand, sucking his index finger as feverishly as she had sucked his member.

He groaned against her, sucking her clit into his mouth, and her body exploded with a release that went on and on as he continued to tease and suckle her until she thought she would black out if he didn't stop. Abruptly, he moved over her, gasping harshly as he aligned his body with hers and thrust. She cried out, arching upward and reaching for him, clutching his arms.

He covered her mouth with his own, capturing the cries she couldn't seem to stop, was hardly even aware of and she wound her arms around his neck, holding herself tightly against him as he plunged inside her with hard, deep, rapid thrusts. Her body erupted into another shattering climax as he went still, tensed, shuddering as he found his own release.

They collapsed weakly on the bed in a tangle of arms and legs, gasping for breath, stroking each other as their bodies slowly returned to normal. Shivering as the sheen of moisture on her skin cooled, Khalia moved closer to him, placing a kiss above his heart. He cupped her head in one hand, wrapping his other arm around her shoulders and holding her close.

"I was too loud," she whispered self-consciously.

He chuckled. "There is little point in whispering now, sheashona. Next time I will bring a gag. You sounded like a howling garshon."

She pinched him playfully. "I was *not* that loud," she growled irritably. "And, anyway, it was your fault."

He pulled away from her. Pushing her back against the pillows, he levered himself over her until his chest was press against her breasts, his lips hovering just above hers. "I am not convinced. I think I should try again ... just so that we can be certain on this point."

Khalia chuckled. Draping her arms around his neck, she lifted her head, closing the short distance and kissing him lightly on the lips. "You can do anything you like to me, any time ... so long as I can do anything I like to you."

He lifted his head and studied her for a long moment, his expression serious now. "I am your man, Princess. You have only to ask and if it is within my power, I will do it."

Khalia stared back at him for several moments and finally looked away. "But I didn't see your petition among the others," she said quietly.

He stiffened. Finally, he pulled away from her and rolled back against the bed, draping one arm across his eyes. "It would not be accepted."

Khalia came up on one arm, staring down at him. "I would accept it."

He lifted his arm from across his eyes and looked at her for a moment and then reached for her, pulling her across his chest and kissing her deeply, with a slow thoroughness that left her gasping for breath. And when he broke the kiss, he slipped his hands beneath her arms and pulled her up until her breasts swayed before his face, kissing each in turn, teasing her breathless until she was as needy for him as if he had not already thoroughly pleasured her. She braced her palms on the pillow on either side of his head, arching her neck, her eyes squeezed tightly to help her hold the sensations inside of her, to relish them to their fullest.

He slid his hands down to her waist, pushing her back, lifting her hips until their bodies were joined once more, and then guiding her until she found a rhythm of movement that brought her the most pleasure. He stroked her back as she moved on top of him, his hands gentle, loving, as he brought her once more to the peak of ecstasy and found his own heaven.

It felt like good bye.

She was afraid to ask, afraid to say anything at all that might prompt him to say something she couldn't bear to hear.

Replete, they collapsed on the bed side by side, gathering their strength, struggling to catch their breath. Finally, Khalia rolled over half on top of him, slipping one leg between his and resting her head on his chest.

She was half asleep when she felt him carefully disentangling himself from her. She sighed, tempted to ask him to stay, if only for a little while, but she knew the longer he stayed the greater the risk that they would be caught together.

He had not said that he would petition. He hadn't had to. His silence was enough to tell her he had no such intention, and she was suddenly angry with herself that she'd allowed it to pass without remark, made love to him again when he'd all but said she didn't mean enough to him even to try.

She was almost as angry with herself that she'd brought it up at all, fearing even so little was demanding enough to push him away.

The fear grew inside of her that she'd been right, that the poignancy of his lovemaking was his way of saying goodbye.

She wasn't certain how long he stood beside the bed, staring down at her, but finally he turned, gathered his belongings and left. She relaxed fractionally, but found she couldn't sleep. Finally, she got up and went into the bath, allowing the water to pour over her until it slowly cooled.

When she emerged from the bath toweling herself dry, she heard the excited chatter of the sheashona in the sitting room. Frowning, she pulled a gown on and went out to see what had excited the little bird. A serving woman was setting a tray on a table near the couch. "What are you doing here?" Khalia demanded.

She startled the woman, who nearly knocked over the goblet that sat on the tray. Steadying it, she glanced up at Khalia. "I beg your pardon, your highness. I thought you might want something to eat before bed. I couldn't help but notice you ate little at dinner."

Khalia eyed the woman suspiciously. Her face was unfamiliar … which didn't necessarily mean anything. She was surrounded by so many servants, she might easily have overlooked a dozen or more. She wondered, though, why and how the woman would have had the opportunity to observe her at the state dinner. "You were there?"

The woman shook her head. "I was helping in the kitchen."

She seemed anxious to leave, sidling closer to the door even as she answered. Finally, Khalia waved her away. "Thank you. You can go now."

When the woman had gone, she made her way to the cage, speaking soothingly to the little bird. It settled down after a few minutes and began to sing. Khalia shook her head. "Why were you upset? This room is filled with people more than its quiet."

Dismissing it, she moved to the tray and saw that the woman had brought a piece of cake and a goblet of wine. Some late supper! Taking the cake, she crumbled a few pieces from it and sprinkled them in the cage for the bird.

The bird hopped from its perch immediately and began gobbling down the crumbs. Khalia laughed. "You are a greedy little thing! I fed you only a little while ago."

She was on the point of turning away when the little bird staggered. It shook its head, opening and closing its tiny beak a couple of times, as if trying to speak and finally fell over on its side, beating its wings against the bottom of the cage. Khalia stared at the bird, too stunned even to think for several moments. Horror dawned as it struggled to drag in a couple of breaths of air and went still.

"Poison." She looked down in horror at the crumbs that still clung to her fingers. Finally, she turned and ran to the entrance to her suite and jerked the doors open. The two men on guard glanced at her quickly, stiffening. "Princess?"

She stared at the men, swallowing with some difficulty as she realized she didn't recognize either man. "The servant who was just here. Find her."

The guard she'd spoken to glanced from her to the other guard. "We are forbidden to leave our post, your highness."

Khalia bit back an angry retort with an effort, but she knew the woman had had plenty of time to disappear. It was doubtful, even if the guards weren't a part of the attempt on her life, that either one had done more than glance at the servant. Finally, she stepped back inside and slammed the doors, bolting them. She didn't care what they might think of it. She didn't care if they reported it. She knew they would, regardless of their loyalty. She could not move, or blink, or spit without every movement being reported … and yet another assassin had walked into her room without hindrance.

Crossing the room to the bird cage, she took the bird out and looked down at it in her palm, stroking its still breast. The first sob that tore from her throat was almost startlingly loud in the silence of the room. Covering her mouth with her hand, she took the little bird and disposed of it, and then disposed of the contents of the tray. When she'd finished, she fell into bed and cried until she was too exhausted to cry anymore.

Chapter Eighteen

"What has happened to your little songbird, your highness?" Guiteanna gasped in surprise.

Khalia didn't turn. Instead, she studied the reflection of the room behind her in the mirror, watching the faces of the women who were once more firmly ensconced in her sitting room. "I set her free," she said.

Guiteanna turned to look at her in surprise and finally smiled. "I'm so glad you did. I didn't like to say anything, for I could see you loved it dearly, but it's considered bad luck to capture one. They are meant to be free. It's name means 'joyful sorrow'. It's said that it will bring both to anyone who captures it."

Seeing nothing more than mild curiosity, or boredom, in the faces of the women, Khalia looked down at her hands, wondering now why it was that Damien called her sheashona. She'd thought it must be because of the fiery comb atop its head. Now she wondered if it wasn't because he had sensed that she would bring him nothing but sorrow.

He had not dwelt upon his anxiety about his brother, but she'd seen how close he and his brothers were and she knew he feared his brother was dead already and beyond his help. She'd told Damien that it wasn't his fault, that he hadn't sent his brother into danger. Nigel had made his own decision. She knew, though, that it was her fault.

Her coming had turned their entire world upside down. She saw it every day as she met and spoke with people, saw in their eyes the fear that things would become worse for them and their families.

The coronation was less than a week away. She wondered if she would live to see it, or die shortly afterwards of some strange malady. She supposed she shouldn't have gotten rid of the poisoned food, but what could she have done with it? Offered it was proof that somebody wanted her dead? It could be anybody. The fact that a servant had delivered the tray made it unlikely that it could be traced back to anyone in particular. If she'd caught the servant, things might have been different. The woman could've been questioned. Very likely, she would've eventually told everything she knew--

but then she might have known nothing. Anyone could have handed her the tray.

She wasn't even certain of whom she could trust any longer. The maids blatantly spied on her. She could get rid of them and bring in others, but there wouldn't be a lot of point to it as far as she could see.

Coming to a decision at last, she turned to the maids lounging about the room. "I have a head ache. I'd like to be alone."

The women exchanged curious glances, but none of them wanted a repeat of the previous day and they rose and gathered their baskets of embroidery and books and began to file out of the room. Guiteanna hurried to collect the last of the garments Khalia had discarded the night before and rushed into the bedchamber to put them away. Watching the last of the women file out, Khalia followed them and locked the door, then turned and followed Guiteanna into the bedchamber.

"How did you come to be selected as one of my chamber maids?" Khalia asked, closing the door to the bedchamber behind her. Guiteanna threw her a startled look and finally put a finger to her lips.

Khalia frowned, surprised by the gesture and even more surprised when Guiteanna rushed toward her. "Do not speak loudly, your highness. There are most likely listening devises in the room."

Khalia wasn't certain she believed her. It was true that there were many mechanical marvels in this world that stunned her, but she couldn't imagine how a devise might be invented merely to listen.

"I always scan for them in the mornings when I come, but I was late this morning," she whispered. When Khalia said nothing, she dug into the pouch that hung at her side. Extracting a slender box-like device, she pressed a small button on one side and began walking about the room, waving the device around while Khalia watched her curiously.

When she'd finished, she went into the bath and performed a similar ritual. Finally, she returned, shoving the device back into the pouch, a look of relief on her face. "I didn't find anything," she said quietly. "But I still haven't checked the sitting room."

Khalia moved to the bed and sat down. "Every morning? You mean to say that someone has been putting these .. . listening devices in my apartment ever since I've been here?"

Guiteanna nodded. "Lord Bloodragon sent me to watch over you."

Warmth spread through Khalia instantly at the sound of his name, but she studied the girl carefully for several moments before she spoke, wondering if she dared allow herself to be convinced only because the girl had mentioned Damien. It seemed more than probable that someone had noticed her preoccupation with him, and even if they hadn't, they had every reason to believe that she would trust Damien far more than anyone else. Still, the girl seemed genuine enough, and open enough. It was hard to look upon a face of such innocence and believe the person possessing it was capable of subterfuge, particularly murderous subterfuge. "I'm not certain I can trust anybody," she said wryly.

"You can not doubt General Bloodragon!" Guiteanna exclaimed, and then blushed. "Oh. You meant me?"

Khalia shook her head. "I've no reason at all to distrust Damien. He could have killed me at any time. And I felt that I could trust you even before you said he'd sent you. Otherwise I wouldn't have approached you at all." She rose from the bed and began pacing. "Someone tried to poison me last night."

Guiteanna turned as white as a sheet. "You're certain, your highness?"

Khalia swallowed against a knot of sorrow at the memory. "I fed the sheashona cake that had been brought to me ... I'm certain."

Guiteanna looked around the room as if searching for a place to sit down. "I don't understand it, your highness. Nothing is to be given to you without first being tested. The guards would have communicated with the kitchen and checked to see before they even allowed her to enter your suite."

Khalia shrugged. "Perhaps someone sprinkled poison over it between here and the kitchen. Or maybe the guards were a part of it. When I rushed out to tell them to look for her, they refused to leave their post … and neither man was one that I'd seen before."

Guiteanna frowned. "They can not leave their post--for any reason. Anyone who did would be executed forthwith. They would have raised the alarm, however, or summoned someone to search for her."

Again, Khalia shrugged. "I didn't tell them what had happened. I was … distraught. I suppose I wasn't thinking clearly."

Guiteanna nodded her agreement, then glanced at Khalia self-consciously. "That's completely understandable, your highness."

Khalia frowned. "It infuriates me that that worm thinks he's gotten away with two attempts on my life."

Guiteanna developed a sudden interest in her hands and Khalia looked at her suspiciously.

"There were others?"

She nodded. "At least one. That's why General Bloodragon ordered that you were not to be served anything, not even so much as a glass of water, that had not been tested. Ordinarily, the testing is done only randomly. But one of the cooks was found dead and General Bloodragon did not feel comfortable about the swiftness in replacing him. The food was checked and found to contain poison … which is also why he arranged to have me become one of your ladies … so that he would have some to test the food and drink when it arrives."

"And to look for listening devises."

Something flickered in her eyes, but she nodded readily. "It's not as if you discuss state secrets here, but he didn't want them to know at any given moment exactly where you were and what you were doing or planned to do."

"I doubt there's much my 'ladies' miss," Khalia said wryly.

"No," Guiteanna said slowly, "but you don't trust them
and are always careful what you say around them ... at
least when I've been around. Of course, you might trust
one more than another, speak more frankly with them
when I'm not around. Which I suppose was the reasoning
behind the listening devices, the hope that you might trust
someone enough to tell them things worth hearing."

Khalia smiled at her. "I don't really know why I felt the
need to talk to you--I guess because I needed someone to
share my fears with--I'm glad, though. It's a comfort to
know that I've got someone watching over me."

Guiteanna curtsied. "You have more people watching
over you than you know, your highness."

* * * *

Despite her fears the night before that Damien would not
come to her again, as the evening drew in Khalia convinced
herself that he would. Somehow, he would sense that she
needed him. Somehow, he would know that another
attempt had been made on her life. She sent the women
away as she had the night before, but although she paced
the room for hours and lay awake much of the night, he
didn't come.

She told herself that it was just as well that he hadn't.
There was no sense in taking such risks, and nothing to be
gained, really, by telling him about it now. They had not
succeeded and, if not for pure luck, there would have been
nothing he could have done for her even if he'd been there.

She would just have to trust that they would not try to
poison her again, or that the testers would catch it even if
they did.

The following day, the ladies were all a twitter with news,
which they discussed openly in front of her, about a maid
who'd committed suicide by leaping from the roof of the
palace. Both fear and sickness welled inside of Khalia. She
did her best convince herself that it was merely a
coincidence, but she knew better. The maid had not jumped
unless being picked up and thrown over could be
considered 'jumping'. It was almost certainly the woman

who'd brought her poison, and the small possibility of tying her to the conspirators had thus neatly been disposed of.

She needed Damien, desperately, but she could think of no way to contact him.

When several days passed and she saw nothing of him at all, even during the day, she ceased to seesaw back and forth between anger and worry and endured anxiety alone. Finally, afraid she would give their relationship away, but too worried to contain her fears any longer, she broke down and asked Guiteanna if she knew anything about his whereabouts. Guiteanna had heard nothing either.

She finally decided that Damien had either left the palace to follow up some lead regarding his brother, or that he had left the palace because he needed to put some distance between them.

That thought almost made her hopeful. Surely, she thought, there must be something more to his feelings for her than pure lust, or even respect for her as his future queen if he found it so difficult to stay away?

It brought her little enough comfort, however. She scanned the petitioners for her hand daily in the hope that his name would appear. It didn't, but both her suitors and her ministers became more and more insistent that she make a decision. She finally announced that she had made one. She would not chose a consort until after the coronation.

No one seemed very happy about it, but it seemed the fact that she'd made a date to make a decision was enough to satisfy them at least for a little while.

She found it difficult even to remain coolly polite to her uncle after the poisoning attempt. He'd had the gall to ask her about her little songbird. She'd told him the same story that she'd told her ladies, that she'd set it free.

She supposed she had, but it made her ill thinking about it and she found it very difficult to eat afterward, regardless of Guiteanna's reassurances.

She was almost relieved when the day of her coronation finally arrived. Tensions had wound to a fever pitch as servants rushed frantically about seeing to the last minute disasters and making certain everything was ready.

Her maids woke her at dawn the day of the coronation, torturing her for hours over her toilet. Finally, feeling like a throbbing mass of pain from having been scrubbed and buffed and pinched and pulled, she breathed a sigh of relief as she left her suite and was joined by her escort.

The crowd waiting outside the palace roared deafeningly with approval as she stepped through the entrance and onto the stone porch that fronted the palace. Their enthusiasm was almost more frightening than it was thrilling, but as she stared out over the crowd of faces, she realized she felt much the same swell of pride that she'd felt when the army had come to support her. Almost certainty, there were many among them who'd come merely for the spectacle and the entertainment. Just as certainly, there were those among them who hated her as her uncle did and those who doubted her, but she saw gladness, as well, relief, tears, and she knew that many had come because she'd given them hope that she would change things for the better.

Maybe, she thought, this *is* where I belong.

She lifted her hand and smiled and waved at them, and the crowd roared with approval once more, louder, almost deafeningly. Slowly, she descended the steps and was helped into an open craft that hovered mere inches above the ground. The royal guard fell into formation around her and the other vehicles that made up the procession and the vehicles began to move slowly forward as the army parted the crowd before them.

They arrived at last at the temple of the gods nearly an hour later. Khalia's face felt numb from smiling. With relief, she climbed from the vehicle and made her way up the towering stairs and into the cool, dim interior of the temple. The coronation itself was interminable. The high priests chanted and waved burning incense around while she knelt until her knees felt as if the bones would break through the skin and her back felt as if it would snap.

They prayed over her for hours, or so it seemed. Finally, the crown was brought out and set carefully on her head.

The cape she'd worn was removed and another, much like the one she'd worn to the state dinner, was fastened at her shoulders in its place. She was helped to her feet then and turned to look out over the witnesses that had been allowed to enter the church.

They rose and knelt almost as one, pledging their loyalty to her as their queen.

Her uncle was among them.

She studied him pointedly for several moments and finally strode from the temple and out onto the high porch. If she'd thought the crowds enthusiastic before, it was nothing compared to the wild jubilation that met her when she stood before them once more, crowned as their queen.

The party entered the vehicles once more and they retraced their path to the palace. A feast awaited, a seemingly endless stream of speeches followed and finally Khalia was allowed to retire to her apartments to rest and prepare for the coronation ball.

As tired as she was, Khalia found it difficult to rest. She was certain that Damien would not fail to appear at the ball. She declined any interest in dancing, instead watching the guests in their colorful attire and jewels as they swirled about the dance floor.

It was nearing midnight when she finally realized that Damien would not be coming after all and she found she had lost all interest in the ball.

A fear, barely acknowledged grew inside of her as the night wore on, for she found it impossible to believe that Damien, who had fought so hard to see her settled on the throne of Atar, would not have made an appearance either at the coronation or the ball.

Something had to be wrong … very wrong.

Chapter Nineteen

As exhausting as the day of her coronation had been, it was barely daylight when Khalia's maids arrived the following morning. Bleary eyed, Khalia struggled from the bed. She was only slightly more awake when she'd finished her bath, and wondered how she would make it through an entire day of court … her first as the ruler of Atar.

She was sustained only by the fact that she was to meet with Samala that afternoon in her private office. If anyone knew where Damien was, he would almost certainly be that person. If he didn't, then he would know who she could trust to help her.

The morning was spent settling petty disputes between neighboring lords, most of which were too trivial in Khalia's mind even to have made it through the petitioning process. By the time they broke for the mid day meal, she was beyond irritable. Instead of eating, she went to her apartments to rest, tempted to beg off the afternoon hearings.

She might have, except that she had not liked the smug look on her uncle's face when she'd left. She was certain he had something very unpleasant in store for her. She had no idea what that something might be, but she meant to find out.

The afternoon began innocuously enough with a handful of the petitions that had not been heard earlier in the day. The moment the last of them had filed out, however, her uncle stood, bowed and offered her the same smug smile that he'd given her earlier.

"Your highness. We have a matter of treason to consider."

Khalia's heart skipped a beat. She sat forward in her throne. "Who is the accuser and who is the accused?"

Maurkis bowed again and signaled to one of the guards at the door near the back of the room. There was a brief scuffle and guards began to file into the room. At the center of the group, bound in heavy chains, was Damien.

Khalia thought for several moments that she would faint, or be violently ill as she stared at Damien's battered body.

"I, Maurkis Gildwing, charge General Damien Bloodragon with treason against your majesty," her uncle announced, his tone almost gleeful.

Khalia found for several moments that she couldn't even think of anything to say. It took an effort to drag her eyes from Damien so that she could gather her wits. "What is it that you are claiming he has done?" she asked finally.

Maurkis' eyes gleamed. "It is not merely a claim, your majesty, but a fact, and one which has many witnesses. On the night of fourteenth Junus, General Damien Bloodragon was observed entering an empty suite which adjoins your own. When the guard rushed to investigate, he was discovered in a secret passage, fully armed. He has refused to admit his intentions, but the facts speak for themselves. He was armed. He was discovered trying to enter your apartments clandestinely. His intention was to murder you as you slept."

The room erupted into an uproar. Perhaps half shouted that the accusations were absurd. The rest were just as vocal in condemning Damien and demanding his blood. Khalia stared at Damien as he lifted his head and caught her gaze. Ever so faintly, he shook his head.

She knew he was telling her not to admit their affair. She just wasn't certain why and it was that that held her for agonizing moments, unable to think of a response to the accusations. Finally, she signaled to the guards to bring order. "He was there because I summoned him," she said when the room had quieted.

Maurkis gave her a look of feigned surprise. "You'd summoned him, your majesty? To come to your room clandestinely … in the middle of the night after you'd sent your ladies away?"

Khalia's eyes narrowed, but she couldn't prevent the blush that rose to her cheeks. Not that she gave a damn what he thought, or any of the others for that matter, but she knew Damien would not appreciate her blackening his reputation and her own if there was an alternative.

"Since I trusted no one else and knew at least some of my 'ladies' were there to spy on me, yes. Two attempts were made to poison me. One attempt had already been made on my life even before I arrived at the palace. Damien has been trying to discover the conspirators."

Maurkis lifted his brows. "Damien? General Bloodragon, you mean."

Khalia's lips tightened. "Yes."

Maurkis shook his head, pretending confusion. "I'm afraid I don't understand, your majesty. You said the assassins had been sent by the Baklen, that General Damien had discovered that before he even brought you to Caracaren. As for the attempts to poison you here, in the palace … Why have I heard nothing about these attempts? Why were they not reported immediately?"

Khalia cast around a little desperately, trying to think of anything that might help to support her accusations, fighting the temptation to accuse her uncle. She had no proof against him and at least half of the members seemed inclined to support him. She sensed that this would not be a good time to attempt to have him arrested and she suspected he knew very well that she was still too uncertain of her power to do anything. "Send for my maid, Guiteanna. I spoke to her about the attempt to poison me. It was she who told me of the previous attempt."

She settled back when a guard had been sent to find the maid, trying to calm her jittery nerves, trying to jog her weary, frightened mind to think of what we might do. She could not think of much beyond the horror that she had been dining, dancing and celebrating while they'd been torturing Damien to confess to a crime he'd never intended. Why hadn't she tried harder to discover what had happened? Why had no one told her? Her maids gossiped endlessly about everything. How was it possible that Damien had been arrested without anyone else in the palace, apparently, having heard of it?

Because Maurkis had known of their meetings. He'd set a trap and they'd fallen right into it.

And it was her fault. Damien had tried to warn her there was danger in their liaison, but she'd refused to accept it.

She'd encouraged him to risk it, practically demanded it of him.

Relief flooded her when Guiteanna was finally escorted into the room and shown to the witness box. Maurkis strode confidently toward the box. "Mistress Guiteanna, you have been brought her for questioning regarding General Damien Bloodragon, who is accused of attempting to slip into the princess … I beg pardon, Queen Khalia's bedchamber to murder her in her sleep.

"Queen Khalia has informed us that she had summoned General Bloodragon for the purpose of discussing an attempt to assassinate her by poisoning. What do you know of this?"

Guiteanna glanced timidly around the room, met Khalia's gaze briefly and then looked at Maurkis. "Nothing."

Khalia stared at her in disbelief, too shocked at first to believe she'd heard the maid correctly.

"Nothing? Queen Khalia said that it was you who told her that the attempt was the second of two attempts to poison her. Are you saying the Queen has fabricated the tale?"

Guiteanna looked at Khalia and burst into tears. "I'm so sorry, your majesty. It was nothing like that at all. Damien Bloodragon is her lover."

Maurkis sent Khalia a shocked look before returning his attention to his 'witness' once more. "High treason! You're accusing General Bloodragon of high treason against the people of Atar?"

This time the uproar was unanimously against Damien. There was not one face among them that didn't reflect pure outrage and Khalia finally understood what Damien had warned her of. He'd told her it would not be considered suitable, that the people would not accept him. She knew the moment she looked at him that he'd known from the beginning that it would mean his death … and still he'd never denied her. And still she'd doubted that he cared for her.

There is no tomorrow for us, Khalia.

She felt like weeping. Instead, she swallowed her fear and anguish and signaled the guards to restore order once more.

When the noise had subsided, she spoke again. "Damien Bloodragon is not a traitor. He is a loyal and honorable man. He distinguished himself in battle fighting for my grandfather. He has protected me from all harm. No man in this land has more right to rule beside me. I choose him as my consort."

A deathly quiet settled over the room.

Maurkis feigned outrage. "You can not! Your position as Queen of Atar demands that you marry only one who is your equal. The council will not allow it. The people will not allow it."

Khalia felt like ripping the crown from her head and throwing it at him, but she retained just enough common sense to realize that her position was all the hope that Damien had. Abdicating would not remove the charges against him. It would only make her completely powerless to help him.

She glanced at Damien again, hoping that he would tell her what she could do, what she might say. She saw nothing in his expression beyond acceptance and a warning to her not to interfere.

She looked away. She didn't care what the cost was. She couldn't allow them to execute him. She couldn't even bear to think of the horrendous death they reserved for traitors.

"I have accepted him as my mate. You can not tell me that I can not and I will not allow you to execute the father of my child."

"You are saying now that he has bred his child upon you?" Maurkis demanded.

She didn't know whether he had or not, but she thought the chance was good that he had. She nodded.

A cold smile curled his lips. "The offspring of the traitor will be disposed of in its time."

Someone, one of his supporters, she knew, demanded the traitor's death. Within moments, they were all shouting it. Khalia looked around the room at the men who surrounded her. Slowly, it sank into her mind what Maurkis had said, and what he'd meant.

They would torture Damien to death, slowly, and when her child was born, they expected her to give it up for execution, as well as the spawn of a traitor.

A combination of fear, anguish, and pure unalloyed rage filled her at the decree. She was the Queen. They had made her queen, against her will, forced her to consider the needs of the people of Atar above her own needs and desires. Well, if they would have it that way, then they would have it *entirely* that way. She would not be dictated to by them! They would not tell her what was best for her as if she was no more than a child. They would not kill her mate or touch her child.

Enraged, she rose slowly from the throne. As she did so, she felt a surge of heat and power race through her veins, felt it saturate muscle and tissue, spreading through her until she felt fully capable of rending the lot of them limb from limb. As she looked down upon the council members, she realized with a touch of surprise that she was shifting, growing taller and taller until she was many times the size she was accustomed to. Beneath her, she saw the faces shrink with distance as she grew taller still. As she grew, the cries of rage and demands for blood turned to gasps and cries of shock, surprise and finally terror. She ignored them all, stalking toward the man who'd demanded Damien's death.

"I am your Queen!" she shouted, turning to fix each member of her council with her gaze before moving to the next. "You defy my will at your peril! I have claimed Damien Bloodragon as my mate. One more word disputing my choice, one more suggestion that he be put to death because of my decision, one more threat to my child, and I will have you all executed for treason against your Queen!"

"She has shifted!" someone whispered fearfully.

"It can not be … no female in living memory has fully shifted," someone else whispered.

Surprised, Khalia looked down at herself. Instead of the body she was accustomed to seeing, she saw scales, reptilian legs and arms, lethal claws. Arching her neck, she drew in a deep breath and expelled it. A wall of flame erupted from her throat.

She looked down at the council members once more, a pleased smile curling her reptilian lips. Reaching down, she caught Maurkis with one hand and lifted him up until he was eye level with her. "There is a traitor among us, Maurkis Gildwing. YOU!"

She turned to look at the guards gaping at her and dropped Maurkis among them. "Take him ... and his little songbird," she added, gesturing toward Guiteanna. "Question him until he gives you the names of the others, and when you have them, house them with Maurkis in the prison."

The members of the council stumbled from their chairs and dropped to their knees. "Your highness! Forgive your loyal subjects an error in judgment!"

Khalia's eyes narrowed. She studied them for several moments. "Gladly, so long as you don't make another ... for your next will be the death of you. Go, before I change my mind. I've no need of you now ... any of you."

When the last of them had stumbled from the room, she turned, studying Damien, wondering what he thought of this grotesque form. Slowly, a smile curled his lips. Thrusting the men away who held him now in a stunned, slackened grip, he strode toward her, shifting as he moved, breaking the chains that had bound him. When he reached her, he knelt. Taking her 'hand', he kissed it. *You have never been more beautiful to my eyes.*

Skepticism warred with amusement. *You are not just saying that because I have saved your precious hide?*

He laughed. *Is it precious to you?*

Tears clouded her eyes and ran down her cheeks. *Infinitely, Damien Bloodragon.*

As you are to me, sheashona. I have loved you from the moment I first saw you. And every day since that time I have loved you more.

Khalia blinked her tears back and started laughing. "I'm as big as a house! You are blind, my love, if you can liken me to a sheashona now."

He shook his head. "I see."

The End

Following is an UNEDITED excerpt from the second book in Angelique's dragon series, DRAGONS OF THE DAWN.

Dragons of the Dawn

by
Angelique Anjou

Chapter One

There was a full moon tonight, but that only meant deeper shadows for their quarry to hide … or lay in wait for them. MP Cpl. Josephine Benate pressed the button on her radio. "You see him, Murphy?"

Static greeted her when she released the button. "GI piece of shit issue," she muttered, wondering if her partner had gotten out of range or if the buildings were interfering. She pressed it again. "Murphy? What's your position?"

"…end of the field. He's gone over the wire. Heading for the trees."

"Where's our backup?" Again, the response was a burst of static. "Murphy. Where's our backup?"

"I'm on it."

She could tell from his voice that he was running. She cursed under her breath. "Hold your position, private."

He didn't respond. "I say again, hold your position for back up."

She scanned the perimeter and the field beyond it and caught a glimpse of movement just outside the fence. She knew it had to be Murphy and wondered if he'd called for backup, as he'd been ordered to, before he ditched their jeep. She had a bad feeling he hadn't. She ought to have known better than to leave it to him. He was too gung ho for his own good. "Stupid rookie," she ground out and began jogging in his direction, scanning the area between her partner and the edge of the woods.

A shadow detached itself from the ground and bolted for the woods. He wasn't twenty feet in front of Murphy. Josie ran faster, hoping to avert disaster. She almost ran right past the break in the fence. Skidding to a stop, she doubled back and pushed through the cut wire. The cut edges scraped across the sleeve of her uniform and snagged, jerking her to a halt. She grabbed the wire with her other hand and gave it a yank to free herself. As she did, she heard a meaty thud behind her. "Damn it!" she growled, pulling against the snag so hard she staggered when she finally came loose.

Whipping her head around, she scanned the clearing and zeroed in on the two men struggling near the edge of the woods. She launched herself into a full out run. She was within a couple of yards of the struggling pair when the report of a pistol almost defended her.

She didn't know if Murphy had fired, if the suspect had managed to get Murphy's pistol, or if both men had a gun, but she didn't have time to retreat. Without taking time to consider it, she launched herself into the air, diving for them.

As if watching the event in slow motion, she saw Murphy crumpling toward the ground. She saw their suspect's mouth working in a silent yell and his head turning in her direction, watched as he brought his gun arm up.

Her impact with the suspect stunned both of them. Two seconds after their midair collision, they hit the ground. Josie rolled and came back up on her feet, scrabbling to pull her own weapon from its holster. The suspect, she saw, was on his feet, as well, and no longer armed. He glanced quickly around for his weapon and dove at her instead. He hit her so hard the weapon she'd just pulled from her holster went flying off into the darkness, pinning her to the ground, he shoved his forearm under her chin, pressing against her throat.

A roaring filled her ears. She clawed uselessly at his arm for a moment and then went for his eyes. He jerked his head back beyond her reach, but the movement also relieved the pressure on her neck. She grabbed the arm he was trying to choke her with, pushing up on it and bucked, trying to throw him off of her. Grinning, he grabbed both of her wrists and shoved her hands into the dirt, scooting up far enough he could put a knee of each hand.

She jerked the first hand from beneath his knee while he was trying to secure the other with his opposite knee. This time, instead of going for his eyes, she went for his crotch, grabbing a handful of cods and squeezing them for all she was worth. He let out a high pitched scream and grabbed for her hand with both of his, trying to pry her fingers loose. Balling her freehand into a fist, she drove it upwards with all her strength into his nose. Blood gushed down his face. She managed to buck him off of her while he was distracted and scrambled to her feet, but she'd barely gained her feet when he launched himself at her again.

She leapt to one side, but not far enough or fast enough. He managed to catch hold of the leg of her trousers and jerk her off balance. She drew her knee up and caught him on the side of the head with her boot, stunning him long enough to scramble for to her feet.

He was already on his knees by the time she'd regained her feet and whirled to face him again. Something caught her eye as she turned to face her assailant, but it didn't register in her mind immediately. She was too intent on immobilizing the suspect before he managed to find one of the pistols. Even as she drew back and kicked the man in the ribs with the toe of her steel toed boot, it clicked.

There was a man behind her … and it wasn't Murphy.

She leapt over her suspect, whirling so that she could see the other man. She only caught a glimpse of a whole lot of naked flesh, however. Despite the cracked rib she knew she'd given him, the man she'd kicked was on his feet again almost before she landed on the other side of him. She discovered she'd lost her hat in the scuffle when the man caught a fistful of her hair, nearly pulling it out by the roots as he used it to swing her around.

Ignoring the pain that brought tears to her eyes, Josie used the momentum her assailant had given her to drive her elbow into his cracked rib. Her elbow immediately went numb, but the man released his grip on her hair as he doubled over and spat blood.

She backed off, flexing her fingers to try to get the feeling back. "You're under arrest, Sergeant Collins," she said gustily. "Put your hands behind your back, soldier!"

Slowly, he straightened, swaying slightly.

"Get down on the ground and put your hands behind your back."

"I don't think so," Collins ground out, leaping toward her again.

Josie bounded into the air, launching a flying kick at his head. Pain shot through her knee and ankle at the impact, but his head jerked sideways, changing his trajectory. He plowed up the dirt to her left. Josie landed in a half squat, ground her teeth against the pain and pushed herself upright, glancing from Collins to the stranger, who hadn't so much as moved a muscle. "Who are you and what are you doing here?" she demanded, keeping her eye on Collins, who'd struggled to his knees.

The stranger still didn't answer. She flicked a glance at him, saw that he still hadn't moved and strode toward Collins, kicking him hard enough on the ass that he plowed dirt again.

She dared another quick glance at the stranger and finally decided he must be an escaped mental patient. She couldn't think of any other explanation for his being here stark naked ... and as far as she could see, he was.

She didn't think he could be Collins' contact, in any case. He seemed unthreatening, at the moment, at least. She divided her attention between the two men while she felt around for her handcuffs. The distraction cost her. As she clamped the handcuff on one of Collins' wrists, he rolled, throwing dirt in her face and pitching her over him. She managed to tuck herself into a roll as the ground zoomed up to meet her. Coming up on her feet again, she whipped around to face Collins.

That was when she discovered he'd managed to get one of the pistols ... and he had it aimed at her head. She dove away a split second before he fired, but she had no where to run and she realized she wasn't going to be able to reach the trees before he put one in her back. She made the attempt anyway. The second bullet caught the edge of her trousers, searing the skin.

The third bullet brought a gurgling yelp from Collins. The sound caught her attention and she whirled to look. The naked stranger had one hand on Collins' gun arm. This wrist was dangling at a sickening angle, the pistol hanging from one finger now.

Josie stopped, staring at the two men, wondering how the stranger had managed to cover so much distance so fast. When he released Collins, the sergeant crumpled to the ground, nursing his smoking boot.

After a moment, she moved cautiously toward the two men. "Who are you?" she demanded again.

The stranger, who'd been studying her from the moment she changed directions and headed toward them, spoke for the first time. "Lord Nigel Bloodragon, Duke of Sarcen."

Josie stopped abruptly in her tracks. She'd been right to begin with. The man had to be a mental patient. The problem was, they were miles from any mental hospital that she knew anything about.

She couldn't see it in his eyes … but then there wasn't that much light. Still …. Now that the adrenaline had stopped pumping through her bloodstream and the shock was beginning to wear off, she saw he wasn't completely naked as she'd thought. He was wearing something like a jock sock--she'd gotten a glimpse of one butt cheek so she knew it was a thong. It looked like the sort of thing a male dancer would wear, particularly in light of the fact that the man had he muscular physic of a body builder. For that matter, his whole getup almost shouted male dancer--or maybe he was some kind of S&M nut? There were epaulettes on his shoulders that looked as if they were made of metal. There were one to two inch spikes poking out from the epaulettes. Some sort of filigreed metal curled around his ribs, joined in from just above the jock sock, and he had one hell of an impressive package tucked into that thing. Either he had the balls of a stud bull, or a cock like one. A dark cape fluttered behind him. He also had about a thirty inch sword tucked into a scabbard at his side, but he'd made no attempt to draw it and she thought it might be just for show.

Who did he think he was, anyway? Super cock?

"Step away from my prisoner."

He looked down at the man at his feet and finally stepped away from him. She moved toward the men cautiously. That was when she realized 'super cock' was somewhere between six and seven feet tall.

"Back off," she ground out, suddenly wishing she had her revolver…or two dozen MPs with automatics at her back. The guy wasn't just a giant. He moved like greased lightening. She'd been between the two men when Collins started firing, but he'd still managed to close the distance and break Collins' wrist before Collins got off his third round.

A docile as a lamb, the hulking giant moved a few paces further, but not nearly far enough to suit Josie. Texas might have been far enough.

Collins screamed when she grabbed his wrist. She ignored him, putting her knee in his back and cuffing the other hand.

"Bitch! My fucking wrist's broken!" Collins ground out when he managed to catch his breath.

"You're lucky I don't break your fucking neck, you son-of-a-bitch! You shot my partner…. Murphy!" she yelled. "Murphy? Are you all right?"

"That one is dead."

Josie looked at the stranger sharply. He had a strange accent, making it difficult to understand him. Russian, she wondered? "Did you do it?"

He shook his head, pointing to Collins. "That one."

She picked up the pistol that lay in the dirt. "What are you doing here? This area is restricted."

"I came to look for someone to aid me in a just cause. I need a female."

Josie was taken aback. She didn't have another pair of handcuffs though. Holding the pistol leveled at the stranger, she moved to Murphy and checked him for a pulse. There wasn't one. She'd feared as much. He hadn't made a sound since he'd gone down. Shoving the pistol into her holster, she rolled him over. His chest was soaked with blood. Collins had caught him in heart. She swallowed against the knot that welled in her throat, but it was some consolation to know that he hadn't lay dying while she was busy trying to subdue Collins.

She was liable to be facing a Court Marshall, though.

"You're going to fry for this one, Collins," she ground out.

Pulling Murphy's cuffs from his belt, she stood once more and studied the stranger. "You're not going to give me a hard time, are you?"

His brows rose questioningly.

"I'm going to have to take you in, too," she said steadily.
"Why?"

"This is a government facility, and it's restricted. I'll have to take you in for questioning … If nothing else, you're a witness."

He frowned thoughtfully. "How much time will this take?"

Josie gave him a look. "A few hours ... maybe a few days."

"I do not have time ... now. When we return, I will do so."

Josie's heart skipped a few beats. "What are you talking about?"

"You are a soldier, yes?"

Josie nodded. "Military police, sir. Your cooperation will be appreciated."

He shook his head. "This is a strange world. I could scarcely believe you were a female and still a warrior, and yet I have seen your prowess as a fighter."

Josie stared at him in dismay. Just when she'd decided he *wasn't* a mental patient! Where the hell was her backup? Even if Murphy hadn't made the call, *somebody* should have heard the shots that had been fired. The damn place should be crawling with MPs by now. "All righty, then. Let's just take this slowly. Turn around and put your hands behind your back."

"Quick dicking around with the lunatic, bitch! I need a medic. I'm bleeding to death here."

Josie slid a glance toward Collins. "Shut up, asshole. Don't worry about it. I'm not going to let you die. I want to watch when they execute your sorry ass." When she looked at the stranger again, she saw he hadn't moved.

"I should explain," he said slowly. "Our future queen is in peril. We dare not take her to Caracaren, for the traitors await her there and they have already made one attempt on her life. I need a female to pose as the princess while we ferret out the traitors. Be assured that I will protect you from harm."

"I really don't want to shoot you, sir, but I'm going to have to if you don't turn around and put your hands behind your back ... right now."

He tipped his head to one side. "I do not believe that ... pistol? Will operate."

"I figure I've still got at least three bullets. It might not bring a hulking brute like you down, but it'll sure as hell fuck up your day."

"The end is bent," he pointed out, almost apologetically.

Josie's gave flickered down at the gun. "Shit!" Tossing it aside, she sprang into the air, aiming a flying kick at his head. He caught her foot with one hand. It was like hitting a brick wall, immovable. A jolt went through her entire body. She landed on the ground so hard it knocked the breath from her lungs and rattled her brains against her skull. Before she could do more than grunt, he'd scooped her off the ground.

"Are you injured?"

Besides scrambling her brains and breaking every bone in her body? She lifted her head with an effort, trying to focus her eyes … which seemed to be rolling around independently of each other. "Jus.. fine," she managed to say in a slurred voice.

He caught her lolling head and studied her a moment. "You are only stunned. We should go now. I will explain all when we reach Atar."

Cradling her tightly against his chest, he took off at a run. Josie bit her tongue at the first jolt and tasted blood. She clenched her teeth together after that. She'd just begun to feel some of the pain easing off when they went airborne. Before she could do more than gasp in a single breath of air, she felt something cold and slimy crawl over her skin, felt a cessation of movement, and sound. Gelatin?

Panic washed over her, freezing the blood in her veins. Abruptly, the fell through it and movement, sound and air rushed over her. The jolt when they landed made several bones along her spine crackle.

Josie hadn't even realized that she'd squeezed her eyes shut, preparing for impact, until the jolted to a stop. Opening her eyes, she looked up. In the night sky above them, three moons, one full and two half moons, were lined up like the lights on a runway.

Printed in the United States
32133LVS00001B/32